# Where the leaves go

## Viiola may

Copyright © 2021 Viiola may

All rights reserved.

It is during our darkest moments that we must focus to see the light.-
Aristotle

# Nesryn's playlist.

Held down: Laura Marling

Blouse: Clairo

Not Allowed: Tv Girl

Something In The Way: Nirvana

Three Little Birds: Bob Marley& The Wailers

Autumn in New York: Jo Stafford

Back to the Old House: The Smiths

# CHAPTER ONE

"I want you to ask yourself where the leaves go. For this term's summer assignment I want you to write an essay in your own words, where you think the leaves go when autumn comes?" Mr Rossini says as the school bell goes off and everyone screams, "schools out!"

I jumble around all the papers on my desk trying to make an organised pile to shove in my backpack.

"I'm looking forward to hearing where you think the leaves go, Nesryn you've always had a vivid imagination." Mr Rossini says walking up to me handing me the homework sheet as I nod, and get up out of my seat.

"Thank you Mr Rossini, I will try my best!" I announce getting out of my seat and walking out of the class as I give him a brief wave.

Several hours later

I am sat at my desk scrolling through my Tumblr feed. A smutty Bucky Barnes fan fiction pops up. I look at it for a good minute knowing I shouldn't be reading it but I shrug and start at the beginning. I shovel what I'm sure is the hundredth Oreo into my mouth when my sister storms into my room.

"Well come in, why don't you" I snap rolling my eyes and slamming my laptop shut abruptly, hoping she didn't see what I was reading.(OH Bucky Barnes take me now, sex god!)

" Would you listen Ugh, Jared told me he loved me after sex last night!" Bells says huffing out and throwing one of my throw pillows at me as I catch it ignoring what she's saying as she continues to rant on about her love or lack of for Jared.

Isabella has had her heart broken six times this year and we are only in June.

"Get real bells you've loved him about as much as I love Edger!" I announce whilst glaring at her as she giggles.

Edger mum's husband number four, I hate him.

"Don't look so downhearted Nes, you just need to be a little different that's all, you should be a little more like me, guys don't really like the whole shy timid, thick glasses nerdy tom boy kind of spiel," Bella says lecturing me, the exact same lecture she's given me every time she falls at a new guy's feet, which is a lot of times.

Oh please.

So, my hair's a tiny bit messy and knotted and doesn't know if it wants to be ginger or brown. My eyesight well let's just say that isn't fifty, fifty and I raided the charity shops for most of the clothes I wear, but it doesn't mean I'm undesirable.

I think in some ways I am very desirable; I just don't do anything to appear pretty in the public eye.

In my middle school yearbook, I was voted most ugly.

The truth is that I felt ugliest deep down and it showed in the way others viewed me. I had bright pink rubber bands on my braces, glasses that were so tight on my face they left a mark, a variety of mosquito bites on my arms and legs that I had picked and turned scabby, a pimple at the middle of my forehead that never seemed to fade, but my biggest insecurity was.

My mother.

In my high school yearbook, I was voted most likely to end up an alcoholic, once again, thanks mum.

It stung a bit at first but as soon as I turned eighteen things changed. My body changed, men no longer just walked past me. They'd stop and stare at my youthful beauty, my pale Ivory skin staring back at them enticing them. However, never my full Rosie lips because, well my lips were always kind of small especially my top lip. Sometimes the men would admire my blushing complexion and chubby cheeks.

Safe to say my late puberty gave me a bit of a slimmer look, losing the added puppy fat and braces, but it never changed what was inside (as cliché as that sounds),if guys got a hint of my crazy thoughts, they'd run a mile, I'm sure of it.

My father passed away when I was five. He suffered a long painful battle with depression, and decided it was too long overdue so he wrote a long note and left this earth. I still have the note even with the blood splatters.

Isabella and I have different dads. She's three years older than me she's twenty-one and my mother was with her dad for about three years then my mother cheated with my dad and got pregnant with me,
Back then mum was a real go-getter.

Anyway.

It was my fifth birthday and my mother was out shopping and gossiping with the local lowlife suburban mothers who thought the sun shone out of their children's asses.

Isabella was at her dad's for the weekend. I remember the day before being extremely jealous. This is because she said that she always got cotton candy and took to the beach. I loved the beach.

Well moving on. My father put on strawberry shortcake and I sat and watched contentedly. I heard the bang my father took my uncle's hunting rifle and put it in the middle of his head. The contents of his pineal gland splattered on the sofa. It was a couple of hours before my mother got back home.

After that two weeks later, my mother got married to husband number 1 and I got my first therapist.

His name was Paul. He was nasty. I would cry all night afraid of the dark creeping in while he left the door open. He beat my mother senseless. I would scream as the nightmares crept up but no one would come nor would anyone care.

Then husband number 2 Dave. He had a thing about little girls. My mother would leave me with him when she was shopping. He'd make me do catwalks in my mother's French lace underwear if I would refuse. However, he'd hit and pinch me all over and after he left it left a dent in my confidence and spirit. I was 10.

Then there's Ross, husband number 3. Mum had a kid with him, Tay, he's 2, he's sweet actually but Ross, he didn't like me much. He would suggest putting me in a foster home. I was in one for four months when I turned sixteen. He managed to get rid of me at least till he got bored of my mother. They always get bored.

The fourth husband edger, yes he's not the worst, but it would be nice for my mother to pick me, to care about me. I guess it's safe to say I'm to blame for marriage number 4's dissolution.

"Would you stop daydreaming? We have got to go out tonight. Dylan's throwing the sickest party. Everyone's taking vodka. I heard Ella say Jeremy is gonna try and hook up with me" Bells says as I roll my eyes.

I'm pretty sure she said she loved Jared ten minutes ago but what do I know?

"Fine sure, I guess, I will come, but only for the chance to get away from Edger and Mummy dearest!" I say sarcastically smirking at bells as she jumps up and down on the bed like an excited little puppy.

# CHAPTER TWO

"This music is so rad!" Bells announces swaying back and forth along with the music, nodding her head to Nirvana whilst pulling my hand into the circle of the room where everyone is dancing and sweating. I internally cringe Feeling awkward, as some guys from Bell's work dance up to me and tries dancing up close against me, I make my way away from him.

Eww.

"Bella I'm off to get a drink," I say smiling at her as she laughs and sways her long blonde hair to the music.

"Kk beioch." She shouts over the music while grinding up her friends while trying to dance sexily.

I walk into the kitchen, pulling down the tight green dress that Bells lent me in a dull attempt at feeling less self-conscious.

And for a moment, a split second, I forget about my father's death. I feel like a normal teenager with normal friends and normal thoughts that run through my normal head. For example, what mascara should I put on and does that boy even like me?

And then it hits me, my father is dead. I can see him sitting in the leather brown chair in the corner of the room blood pouring from his skull as my five-year-old self cried out for him to wake little did I know he would never wake again.

I'm standing thinking about him when Bella stumbles over to me.

"What's up Ness, you don't want to leave this early again, do you?" Bell says referring to my last two-party attendances.

"No, I was just thinking, let's get hammered let's forget tonight and just drink!" I shout over the music as she takes my hands and jumps up and down with me.

"But you have to remind me to get up at eight because mum said I got to watch Tay because she's invited to Edger's special breakfast talk thing he does at work," I say as she smirks.

"You will be there in time; I mean on time, I mean Scouts honour!" She says stumbling on her words saluting me as I laughed.

I get a cup and pour myself some red wine. I down it instantly and as soon as it hits the back of my throat it's like some sort of switch just clicks. My alcoholic gene kicks in, I get a shot of vodka and down it.

Ten minutes later me and bells are dancing shimmying our stuff clinking red solo cups of God knows what alcohol although I did hear some guy say it's tequila.

Tequila does not taste pleasant!

An hour passes and I'm stumbling around. Soon enough my vision becomes blurry. I wonder if I'm still wearing my glasses. I stumble up the stairs looking for the bathroom. I feel like I'm about to be sick.

"What the hell did I drink bells?" I mumble as she rubs my back while I'm bent over the toilet.

"Everything, hold on, hold that thought!" She says as she takes her hand off me and runs to the bin puking up all the alcohol she drank. The sound of her puking makes me tense up as I puke into the toilet bowl once again.

"You, you know that you are the oldest right? I should be the good example I mean you I mean years older!" I say slurring my words as Bells giggles laying down on the floor.

"Come lay with me Ness, I'm tired." She says as I lay down on the floor and hug onto her.

"Eww, you smell like sick." She says making a funny face.

"How about you, you smell like vodka and tomatoes and tuna sandwiches, you smell grotesque," I say dramatically while she laughs and hits my chest. Soon enough, she's asleep, and I'm drifting away as well.

# CHAPTER THREE

I get up holding my head already feeling the full force of the thumping from the hangover, moving off what looks like a sofa/futon I look around taking in my surroundings, teenage hungover sleeping bodies spread all over the room, I search around and finally find Bells laying asleep on the pool table.

"Bells, mum is going to kill me and not to mention you, we are supposed to watch Tay!" I hissed, shaking her shoulders abruptly, trying to wake her from her very peaceful slumber.

"Can't edger just watch him; I'm trying to sleep!" Bella says rolling over on the pool table and sucking her thumb like a child.

"No Bella, he's at work, come on please, get the fuck up!" I shout losing my patients and pulling her thumb out of her mouth, pulling her up by her arms as she looks around getting her handbag stumbling along following me out the house.

 I open my bag shuffling around all my trinkets finally finding my keys. I get my green 2005 Vauxhall Corsa as Bella gets in the passenger side not wasting any time to leave as we start to drive home.

"She's going to flip, I'm so fucking dead!" I announce as I drive extremely fast, faster than the law of speed limits.

I turn away from looking at Bella as I stop ranting and see a signpost. She screams "Stop!". We crash into it rapidly as my face whooshes directly into the airbag as Bella springs forward in her seat as her seat belt clicks.

"Isabella, hey Bells, get out!" I scream hitting her arm as we get out of the car as fast as possible and the signpost falls onto my car smashing the screen as people beep Bells calmly turns to them, and gives them the finger.

"I'm so dead." I cry sitting on the curb holding my hands to my head.

Me and Bell sit on the curb, Bella being way calmer than me waiting for edger and mother to turn up.

"What the hell!" Mother screams dramatically getting out of edgers expensive grey Audi RS5. I watched Bell's dad get out of his car and run up to her embracing her in his arms.

Sometimes I forget that we have different dads but times like this, they hurt.

"You know how much this is going to cost to fix." Mother shouts getting up in my face.

"I'm okay, thanks for asking June just minor whiplash, but it's nothing like the inconvenience my existence has caused you!" I snap calling my mother by her name rolling my eyes.

"You are out of control, you are drunk; I can smell it on your breath," Mum shouts getting closer to me.

"Like mother like daughter then huh, what's that saying? Apple doesn't fall far from the mother!" I hiss out glaring at her, Mum's hand makes its way to my face, I look at her shock painted on me as I stumble back instinctively, heat rises to my cheek as I hold it feeling the sting from her cold bony hand.

"You are an adult now, you will take responsibility for your issues, if me and Edger want this marriage to work, something has to change." She announces as I stand still, unable to talk from shock.

"You have screwed up, yet again all you ever seem to do is screw up. You are turning into a screw-up, Nesryn!" Edger shouts adding his input like he has some sort of say in my life or even impact on my way of thinking because he says screw up three times.

Ugh, asshole.

Meet Edger, he is my stepdad. He's okay most of the time but he's just kind of plain boring. He's kinda like the stale old dirty biscuit that you leave in the biscuit tin that no one will eat and it stays there for months and then one day you're craving a biscuit so hard and you go in the biscuit tin and there's only that mouldy stale old biscuit that's left, you have to decide whether you want it or you throw it away, well my mother decided she wanted it, unfortunately.

"Me and your mum have spoken to your father's mother!" He says as I interrupt.

"You mean grams Joyce," I say glaring at him. She's not just my dad's mum, she's my grams once again.

Ugh, asshole.

"Yes, and we have booked you a ticket, Isabella will stay with her dad and you will stay with your grandmother until you can come back a mature young woman Nesryn," Edger announces as I glare at him even longer this time like at any second, I'm about to sprout wings and fly over to him smacking him across that overactive mouth of his.

"I'm not leaving," I say quietly to my mother crossing my arms as I watch her take out her emergency stress pills that her therapist gave her after diagnosing her with seasonal depression when she told him she felt empty.

Translation: she ran out of alcohol.

"Nesryn, it's not up for discussion, pack your stuff, your plane leaves in a couple of hours." My mother says. I cringe as I feel the sensation of sandpaper rolling along the back of my tongue as she swallows the pill dry.

"Fine," I say sighing feeling defeated, knowing I'm not about to win this one.

Sure, I couldn't care less about leaving mum and edger but I'd be leaving Tay, my half-brother. Since I let him down, I will not see him for a while. I don't know what's going to happen since when my mom gets drunk and edgers cheats on her after an argument, they don't have the time to take care of him, so me and Bells alternate.

When I'm not around, who's going to care for him?

Who cares for me?

# CHAPTER FOUR

I get off the bus a couple hours after a 7-hour flight.

"Hello, Toronto," I say sarcastically pulling my dark green Beanie off of my head feeling the scorching sun shining down on me.

I start to look around scanning people, when I see a tall blonde girl next to my Nan holding up a sign that says "welcome home Nesryn" .

"Cute," I mumble as I notice the puffy neon green paint they used sloppily. I start walking over to them as slowly as possible savouring my last moments by myself.

"My darling Nessy," Grams says smiling at me as I hug her.

"It's nice to see you, Nan, it's been a while," I say looking at her.

"Come get in the car sweetie let's drive you home, you must be exhausted" Nan says as I get in the back of the car.

"Who's the girl, Nan?" I say looking at the girl driving the car. She's pretty a complete polar opposite of astronomical proportions to me. I have hazel brown eyes, frizzy dark brown curly hair with large glasses, I'm porcelain pale and super short.

The girl has blonde pin-straight hair pretty blue eyes she's skinny with a tall killer figure. She's very tanned. She's every guy's dream model girl.

"This is your cousin Lottie do you remember her? you used to have baths together when we'd come and visit" Nan says.

Always say yes when a family member asks if you remember something or someone. I learned the difficult way by saying no and getting several family members offended.

"Course I do," I say smiling whilst lying through my teeth.

"She lives with me, after her mother suffered through the same thing your mothers have been through," Nan says as I glare at her.

"What serial marriage and alcohol abuse sure must suck for my good old mum seeing as she's only ever caring about herself and husband number four," I say sucking in an aggravated breath as my Nan glares at me.

"If I ever spoke about my mother like that, I'd get a belt to the face," Nan says as I look down and just put my headphones in for the rest of the journey.

"Here we are," Nan says. As I walk into the house it smells like old people and dove soap.

"Where do I sleep, I'm pretty jet-lagged," I say smiling looking at my cousin Lottie.

"Here I will show you!" She says smiling a welcoming smile.

"Thanks," I mumble as I walk up the stairs.

"So, there is my room there's the bathroom we have to share, Nan has her own and there is Nan's bedroom and here's your room." She says giving me the low down on where everything is, she opens the bedroom door and I walk in.

"I like the wallpaper," I say looking at the white walls and blue rose wallpaper covering the walls.

"Thanks, I decorated it last week," Lottie says as I smile.

"I'd get some sleep if I was you before Nan gives you the "you can't live for free talk","" Lottie says quoting Nan as I laugh a bit.

"Thanks for the heads up Lottie," I say as she nods.

"I'm always here if you need anything." She says smiling.

"Same here, I mean for you," I mumble awkwardly.

"I will leave you to get on." She says walking out of my room.

I strip out of my mom jeans and vest top into my Sage green oversized t-shirt and a pair of tartan shorts.

I walk into the bathroom sitting on the edge of the bathtub.

I get my phone out dialling my mother's phone number and shoving my phone charger into a charger port.

"Nesryn," Mum says down the phone as I shiver hearing her cold detached voice.

"June," I said gritting my teeth calling her by her first name.

"Well, I'm glad you made it through the plane ride," Mum says as I roll my eyes.

"Yes, wouldn't it be a shame if I ended up dead with dad where someone actually cares about me?" I say twirling the phone charger around in my fingers anxiously.

"Would you stop with the hysterics already Nes? It's getting old, you know I have to do this to save my marriage to the man I love," Mum says as a tear falls down my cheek.

"Well, mum save marriage number four do all you can to save whatever you need to save

I'm fine just don't call again," I say as more tears fall uncontrollably as I wipe my cheek furiously.

"Stop with the drama already, Nesryn I have to do this, "mum says in her I can't be bothered voice she puts on; God I hate that voice.

"I'm fine, Nan's just great, Toronto's better than London so stop calling, I'm fine I'm fine I'm fine," I shout slamming the phone down on the sink as my hands shake.

I pull out my bag getting my medication, I open the bathroom bin and shove them in there.

They make me numb, what's the point?

# CHAPTER FIVE

"Rule one, you live here you eat what we eat, rule two, you go out on your own or you go out with Lottie, you come back by ten sharp, rule three, you make a mess you clean it up, rule four, you eat when we eat!" Nan says glaring at me, geez my Nan can be scary when she wants to be.

"Anything else?" I question biting into my cookie savouring the taste of the sweet cinnamon sugar.

"Yes, Nessy rule five you must get a job!" She says as I almost choke on my cookie, I watch Lottie giggle.

"Lottie set you up an interview with the family she cleans for, to become their nanny," Nan says as I laugh.

"that's so funny, but I'm not being a nanny gram," I say bluntly as she chuckles sardonically.

"Sweetie, you are missing the point. You don't get a choice. The Robertson family have kindly given you a chance. Like Lottie, you will take it, the interview is tomorrow. I've given Lottie some money to take you into town, to get you an outfit. "I want the change back," Nan says sternly. I roll my eyes.

As I grab my handbag and smile at Lottie, I say, "Fine whatever, are you ready?".

"Yup, let's go." She says kissing my Nan's cheek.

"Are you forgetting something Nessy?" Nan says as I roll my eyes and walk up to her kissing her other cheek.

"See you later girls." She says as we wave goodbye.

"What's it with Nan and rules?" I ask as Lottie laughs.

"It's just the way she was brought up, you will get used to it. It's kind of comforting when you come from a family of people who couldn't or wouldn't care less what you do." Lottie says as I nod in agreement.

"Thanks, but I don't think that's going to happen any time soon. I'm not good at following rules," I say as she rolls her eyes at me and I laugh.

"Oh my god we have got to go to urban outfitters. They do the cutest jeans and you can get some outfits since you only brought bedtime stuff! "Lottie says as I laugh.

"Yeah, because I had it in my head that I'd sleep all day and read my books all night," I say as Lottie parks the car across from the mall and we get out.

Twenty minutes later.

"This is insanely cute." I say turning around in my ribbed long-sleeved blue top and black skinny jeans I just brought." I announce looking at myself in the mirror.

Ten minutes later

"So, tell me about the family" I say as I'm sat in the food court popping a handful of fries into my mouth and then drinking some lemonade.

"Well, there's Emmalynn we just call her Emma the kids mum and Nate's wife," Lottie says as I almost spit out my lemonade.

"Emmalynn and Nate, huh! Very posh Toronto is so weird!" I chuckled.

"he's from London too, well he doesn't have an accent because he moved when he was little!" She says divulging all the information she knows about him to me as I roll my eyes.

"You know I live in a small town called Lily state, not London close but not quite," I say as she rolls her eyes and stuffs her face with her burger.

"Get real Ness everyone who's from the UK in American's eyes is from London!" she says chuckling as I laugh.

"Also, you say Toronto's weird who calls a town a lily state totally oxymoronic!" She says with her mouthful of burger and I can see her chewing like a cement mixer.

"Also, they are super-rich I mean rich as in they cost more than our whole existence! "Lottie says as my eyes go wide with curiosity.

"What do they do?" I ask raising my eyebrow.

"Porn stars," she announces. This time I actually choked on my lemonade and she bursts out laughing.

"I'm just kidding Emma works for a Lawyer firm and Nate, he's a boxer," Lottie speaks whilst smirking.

"Okay, so if I screw up, he's going to beat me the fuck up, glad to know!" I say as she laughs.

"The kid's names are Tate and Lo, Lo's a nickname, it's short for Logan!" She announces as I smile. Cute names.

"How old are they?" I ask.

"Tate's three and Logan's a year old," Lottie says as I wipe the fries grease residue off my fingers with a napkin.

"Oh, one last thing, do not and I mean do not fancy Nate okay, please. He's cute and all but he's kind of a dick!" She says warning me as I laugh.

"Trust me falling is the last thing you have to worry about with me, more like jumping!" I announce sardonically, my mindset on keeping strictly professional until I get time to kill myself.


"We will see." She says smirking at me like she knows something I don't and I just roll my eyes doubtfully.

# CHAPTER SIX

"I am so proud of you, Hunny you look like a beautiful young lady. Sit, I can make you some breakfast!" My Nan says looking at me. All I'm wearing is the black jeans Lottie picked out and my dad's jumper.

"Thanks, Nan, but Lottie's waiting in the car for me. I got to go, don't want to be late on my first day!" I say hugging her.

Five minutes later,

"What's this car get anyway? Like 20 per gallon!" I say mocking and laughing as Lottie rolls her eyes.

"Hey, it's a classic don't mock it." She says laughing as she drives her vintage rusty Chevy truck.

"Truth is, I'm nervous," I say putting my knees up to my face feeling anxiety flow through me.

"Hey, they are going to love you and if they don't, I'm there to talk them into loving you!" Lottie states laughing.

"Well, I wore my lucky jumper so I can't go wrong, it was my dad's so hopefully it gives me luck!" I say smiling looking at my fair isle Nordic pattern cream and green coloured jumper.

"It's cute and trust me you got this!" She says smiling with such certainty in her eyes.

Ten minutes later.

"Okay, so we are here." She announces, as I look up at the massive modern house standing in front of me as my mouth gapes open in shock.

"What are they rich, I thought you were being sarcastic but they are rich like rich, rich," I say looking at the large glassy windows and the prickly rose bushes that stand tall outside the house around the gate.

"That's the first right thing you've said all day considering I let the dig about my car slide!" Lottie says laughing.

"Holy cow, this place is pretent........" I announce being opinionated asp I shut the car door.

"Excuse me," a woman's voice says startling me as I turn around to look at her.

Shit, I blew it already.

"Sorry, I'm just so taken back by the beauty of your home, I was going to say this place is so pretty," I say fake smiling, looking at the tall blonde women."Oh well, thank you sweetie you must be Nesryn." The woman says as her face softens up.

She's dressed in an expensive light cream coloured Armani pantsuit with tall white matching stiletto heels.

Well, who knew a push to her ego was the save I needed? I guess I got lucky in that department.

"Would you be a darling Lottie and when I'm gone would you show dear Nesryn around the house?" Emma says as I take in ore the house that surrounds me feeling a twinge of jealousy at the lux life she has.

I think my whole bedroom back in the UK was the size of their shed.

"Of course, Miss Robertson," Lottie says smiling politely which I, of course, would mock later on in the day.

"So, I did a background check and it came back clear apart from one thing, your father committed suicide when you were five," Emma says almost like I didn't know myself and she's just now announcing it to me.

I look at her helplessly, unsure of what to say.

"Ugh, yes that's true," I say unable to find real posh expensive people words for Im mentally screwed.

"Well sweetie, I have an amazing therapist who has been a huge help. He is wonderful and really works a treat" Emma smiles as I frown, feeling offended for a moment, but then I paste a fake smile on my face.

"That sounds great Mrs. Robertson, thank you," I say as my thick posh British accent comes through.

"There is my man of the hour, my husband Nate," Emma says rubbing her hand up some tall guy's chest as I internally cringe at the PDA. "Hi I am Nate and I am late to work," Nate says looking at his expensive watch on his wrist as Lottie hands me his coffee to give to him.

He tries to take it out of my hand. However, when he takes it his hand slips and he drops it to the floor and I spill it all over my special jumper. I wince looking at my ruined memento from my father.

"Hey what the hell!" I snap sounding louder than I thought I would as I look up making eye contact with the blue-eyed man.

"Nes!" Lottie shouts as I look over at her then down at my stained jumper.

"I mean, shi….I am sorry let me clean that up for you!" I say as rage bubbles in my stomach and I wipe his white work shirt with a rag.

"It's fine." Nate mumbles grouchily pulling the soggy rag from me abruptly as I remove my ruined jumper leaving myself in my black vest top.

"So, Lottie will introduce you to the little ones when they are awake as till then you will need to do house hold chores with Lottie and oh the pool is free for use." Emma says as I smile feeling my anxiety peak whilst looking down at my ruined jumper in my hands.

"Thanks," I mumble turning away from them and walking into the garden.

# CHAPTER SEVEN

Me and Lottie are sat outside with the baby monitor waiting for the kids to wake up from their slumber. We have our feet dangling in the pool as sweat drips down my neck to my shoulder blade from the scorching heat of the summer sun. I'm sitting with my jeans rolled up above my knees, letting my legs float like heavy weights ready to pull me down.

"What an asshole, he didn't even apologise for what he had done, he was the one who dropped the damn coffee!" I speak feeling infuriated as I continue to rant on to Lottie.

"It's fine, hey you got the job you should be happy! "Lottie says smiling finding a silver lining in what feels like the worst day ever.

"But this jumper, it's my dad's. I mean it was the last thing he gave to me because I used to sleep with it because it smelt like him. It means so much to me. It's my comfort, and he ruined it!" I say feeling my heart breaking.

"Hey I will clean it so thoroughly it will look brand new, I promise!" Lottie says looking at me."The Truth is I haven't washed it since dad died because I was too afraid the smell of him would leave or fade." I say as she smiles sadly and hugs me.

"How old is Nate anyway? He looks way too young to have two kids and be married!" I say mentally scolding myself for showing any form of interest in the asshole.

"He's twenty six." She says smirking as I roll my eyes.

"Emma's fucking her therapist!" I blurt out feeling my filter disintegrating as Lottie laughed like a little piglet.

"Oh, Nesryn let me recommend one for you. He's so handsome and muscular even when he bends me over his desk! "Lottie says getting up and caressing my face as I laugh.

I suggest we jump in the pool, it's a bright day! I get up and strip off my jeans and t-shirt, leaving me in my boy shorts and a pink sports bra.

I jump in as the water splashes and spills everywhere; Lottie disappears into the house as I call out for her wondering where she went to.

I shrug and put my head under the water feeling its warmth being heated by the blazing sun.

I used to think maybe one day when I die, I'd become a wave and whenever I was fully content with being deceased and calm, I'd become still and shallow.

I'm laying floating in the pool when my peace is destroyed by the sound of Lottie calling me. I open my eyes and sit up to see a little boy standing holding Lottie's hand. He's in his red and blue spiderman swimsuit and a 1-year-old boy in a paw patrol shorts and tshirt combo."Mind if we join?" Lottie asks smiling cheerfully.

"No not at all, get in it's nice and warm." I say smiling a false smile because at the back of my mind all I can think about is my dear beloved jumper.

"Hi, Nesbyn." Tate says trying to pronounce my name but missing the r and replacing it for a b.

"Hey Tate, hey Lo I'm Nesryn, I'm your new nanny!" I announce as I notice cute small speckles of gold freckles patterned out on Lo's face in the shape of a deformed butterfly. He has pretty ringlet ginger curls that when pulled spring back into place. I watch as he is annoyed by the hair band, pulling his hair as Lottie helps him remove it.

Tate's got blonde hair with an almost touch of white to it with ivory skin and eyes that are a mix of colours brown, green and blue.

Tate jumps into the pool and I catch him as Lottie climbs in with Lo.

"You think we could spend the whole day out here?" I ask Lottie as she nods excitedly and Tate and Lo cheer.

"If you want the kids to get heat stroke, that'd be a great idea." Someone says from behind us. I turn around from looking at Lottie and see Nate standing inspecting us with a cocky grin plastered on his face.

"What are you doing back Nate? "Lottie says swooning and smiling at him as I roll my eyes at her pathetic childlike crush.

"Work was cancelled for the day something about fire alarm safety checks. I didn't really stick around long enough to be told to stay." He announces shrugging.

"Are you coming in for a swim sir?" Lottie questions fluttering her long eyelashes as I can feel myself internally cringing. I glare at Lottie and she simply smirks back at me.

"Okay, okay if you genuinely want me too, just give me a second and I'll be in." He responds smiling a pearly white smile as I glare at him. The need for him to say " okay, okay, if you really want me too" just feels asinine, making out like we forced his arm, no I really don't want you to join, asshole, of course I could never say that so instead I just think it. I watch and notice him starting to unbutton his work shirt and jeans as I turn around, I watch a smirk rise on Lottie's face as she puts her hand to her heart and fakes a beat with her hands like butterfly wings as I roll my hazel brown eyes feeling unamused.

He jumps in and I swim with Tate to the corner of the pool, ignoring his presents and trying to forget about his stupid coffee getting all over my priceless jumper.

Of course, while I'm deep in thought He swims over to me. I just ignore him and continue to play shark with Tate. Tate talks to me in full detail about how his favourite book is There's a shark in the park.

"You don't particularly like me, do you?" Nate says interrupting Tate like he isn't there as Tate swims over to Lottie looking at me as I shake my head.

"I don't particularly know you sir." I say trying to be as respectful as possible, looking at him as I tie my wet hair back out of my face and into a ponytail.

"Come on Nessy, it's Nessy right? You have to chill out because holding all this anger isn't healthy for your soul!" He smirks as I glare at him. He knows he's pissing me off, but is he enjoying it?

"You are not, my family." I snap as he chuckles and dips his head under water then lifts it back up his light blonde hair now a darker shade as he swings his hair in the air like a dog trying to dry its self.

"Oh, how my heart breaks." He states sarcastically smirking at Lottie who on que instantly bursts into laughter like it's the funniest thing she's ever heard.

Two hours later.

"Would you like some lunch? You've been here since nine this morning, you must be starving. "Nate says as I shake my head.

"No thanks, I'm not hungry." I say stubbornly crossing my arms and looking at him bitterly.

"Why are you so pissed off?" He questions like he doesn't know what he has done, as I glare at him.

"It doesn't matter, I'm over it sir I'm just trying to do my job." I say as I pick Tate up and lift him out of the pool as Lottie continues to play with Lo and Nate joins in with them.

# CHAPTER EIGHT

After walking into the house with Tate and drying myself and Tate with an over expensive Burgundy towel Tate sits himself on the sofa and watches some SpongeBob SquarePants. I feel someone brush past me as I look up and see it's Nate getting his white polo shirt on. I roll my eyes as I watch Lottie's eyes glued to him.

"You can borrow a T shirt if you'd like seeing as I ruined your jumper." He says. I look up at him for the first time today really noticing his bright piercing ocean blue eye staring at me.

"Thanks." I say as he hands me a deep green T shirt that looks twice the size of me, but I still take it.

"I meant what I said about being sorry about the coffee." Nate says as I look at him.

"Like I said before, I'm over it." I reply, not looking at him knowing full well I'm lying and I'm not over it.

I sit by the pool with my legs dangled in while I'm sitting in Nate's t shirt and my jeans pulled up.

I hear someone come and sit next to me. I look up and see it's Nate with a bag in his hand, with his jarring smile plastered on his face.

"Lottie told me about how much the jumper means to you, here." He says handing me the bag. I shove my hand into pulling out the jumper. It's clean, not a mark on it. I lift it up to my face and the smell of my father's cologne mixed with cigarette smoke is still present on the jumper. I smile to myself feeling comfort.

"You didn't have to." I mumble quietly looking up at him as he nods.

" I messed up, I wanted to make it right, I couldn't have seen that pretty face of yours frowning all the time." He says looking at me as I smile feeling heat rising to my cheeks.

"Sorry I was so off and moody it's just when my dad died mum, she burned all the photos of him, threw out his clothes his watches his journal, it's like she erased his existence, this is all I got left." I say looking at him as he listens contently.

"Parents can sometimes be selfish." He says softly as he dips his toes in the water and his face contorts into a grimace.

"Oh yeah, it's cold now." I say giggling.

"I will see you round sweetheart." Nate says standing up and walking into the house as I turn to watch him leave.

Sweetheart.

"So how was your first day?" Lottie says smiling as I sit in the front of her car.

"So umm Nate, he is insanely hot like wow!" I say my eyes wide as she giggles.

"I told you, didn't I tell you!" She says laughing loudly.

"Oh, you told me." I laughed.

"His voice when he speaks is so low and sexy, I wonder what his voice sounds like during!" she says smirking at me as I stop myself from picturing him groaning lowly.

"Maybe he's a singer as well as a boxer." Lottie says as I laugh.

"Oh, cool maybe he could put me onto his agent." I say laughing sarcastically.

"I didn't know you sang." Lottie says smiling.

"I do like everyone else in the shower and in the shower only." I say laughing.

"That's it, I'm going to be standing outside the bathroom now every-time you shower to hear you sing "Lottie says smirking as I giggle.

"You know when I got here yesterday, I didn't think I'd like it here, but now it's not the most terrible." I say smiling at Lottie.

"Well, you know Nate has that effect on people." Lottie says as I nod in agreement with her.

"Would it be cool if you just dropped me here?" I say noticing the beach is not too far off.

"Sure, yeah see you at home." Lottie says smiling as I get out the car and wave to her.

Once she leaves, I run to the beach that was about a mile west.

I get to the pier and sit on the edge; I take out my journal.

"Dear journal I've been thinking more and more about how I'm planning to kill myself. I figured drowning would be the easiest and I got to do Toronto some dramatic justice how about a hand full of dark news to gossip about but don't worry I promise there won't be blood, I will make it quick I will be with my dad soon." I write as I put my journal down on the ledge as I look over the railing. I take my jacket off dropping it to the floor shivering as it falls next to the suicide note and my bag.

This is my second option If I don't have the balls to drown, I will die from hypothermia from the cold water.

I start to unbutton my jeans as someone taps my shoulder.

Before I fall over the railing, Nate grabs me in his muscular arms and turns me around quickly.

I look up at him and then move out of grasp.

"What the hell are you doing, Nesryn theirs a no swimming sign right there! "Nate says looking at me as I put my jacket back on.

"Oh, I must have overlooked that what are you doing here " I say, subtly glaring at him and silently cursing him for ruining my plan.

"I come here some times to think." Nate says with his hands in his pockets.

"I should be getting home; I'm just about to look in some of the shops first bye Nate." I say smiling as I walk away from him.

I walk into one of the shops looking at the welcome to Toronto merch. I smile to myself as I look at the hats. I feel someone's presence behind me as I growl and hover my eyes over the dark brown hat, pick it up.

"You know it's going to be really tricky to sneak up on a woman with my foot shoved up your ass!" I snap up turning around to see it's Nate again.

"Nesryn it's me." Nate says as I roll my eyes at him.

"What do you want sir?" I say glaring at him still managing to show some signs of respect for my boss.

"Let me take you home, I want to make sure you get home safely." Nate says as I look at him.

"Sorry but safety isn't really a concern for me okay, I'm fine!" I say as he looks at me like I'm the last puppy at the pound begging to be rescued and I internally cringe

"Please, Emma would be so mad and pissed at me if I let you walk home at this time alone!" He says as I roll my eyes.

"Here." He says taking the hat out of my hands.

"What are you doing?" I say looking at him feeling confused.

"I'm getting you a welcome gift." He smiles as he pays the cashier.

"You fixed my jumper that's more than enough!" I say handing him a five-dollar bill. After releasing my hair from its ponytail, I shoved the hat on my head as I walked out of the shop.

"Fine then say it's from Tate and Logan, but let me take you home." He says handing me the hat and the five-dollar bill back smiling.

"Fine." I mumble following him to his car.

# CHAPTER NINE

"Tell me you did not sleep with him last night in his car, oh my god that's so hot!" Lottie says storming through my bedroom door dramatically as I shut my journal and eyes for that matter.

"For your information he thought I was about to hurt myself and he felt sorry for me so he gave me a lift home. Geez Lottie get your head out of the gutter" I say as Lottie sighs a sigh of relief.

Because she'd want to be the one to get roughly fucked in a car instead of me, yeah can't say I've ever had that urge.

"Anyways Lottie you got to get it out of your head,
"He's my boss, he is our boss. He's not about to sleep with me or you for that matter!" I say laughing as she glares at me.

"Right why are you in such a foul mood? Did you take your bitch pill?" Lottie says sarcastically whilst looking at me.

Well, Lottie since you asked it's because my boss interrupted my easy way out of being alive and made it not so easy.

"Okay so I'm only being honest because you asked!" I say lying looking at Lottie.

"Okay" she says looking at me sceptically and confused.

"I've never been kissed well consensually I haven't let alone anything else. I'm really not that type of girl." I say looking at Lottie.

"The type of girl who sleeps with her super-hot boss and goes at it all night "Lottie says acting like a dog in heat looking at me as I shake my head.

"No, the type to ruin a marriage." I say sighing.

Actually, that's one of the biggest lies I've told since I got here. My mother wouldn't be on marriage number four if I didn't drive them all away.

"Fine but I'm still going to ramble on about how hot he is!" Lottie says laying on my bed.

The next day.

"Ooo let me guess my handbag isn't even This season eww, oh and my chai tea isn't sugar free!" Lottie says flapping as I sit on the kitchen side sipping my bottle of water while the kids are asleep.

"No way, it's more like this." I say jumping off the counter and holding my hand out.

"Susan's sons got the latest Gucci shirt and Tate hasn't, and me and my husband have the most loving relationship ever, oh except for the fact he hates the baby weight I put on because god I just can't stop snacking, but he won't admit it and we have sex once a year and we act like that's a normal thing!" I say strutting and making fun of my bosses as Lottie's face turns bright red like a tomato and she stops laughing and pushes her lips tight together.

"For your information, Miss Nesryn, it's twice a year and I love her baby weight." Nate says as I turn to him and I flush bright red whilst he glares at me. I bite my lip furiously unsure if I want to laugh or cry.

"Um, I ugh you aren't supposed to be back till six." I say as Lottie looks at me like I'm crazy.

Nate says, "Didn't Lottie tell you that I get back for lunch every day from twelve to one" as I glare at her.

"Oh, you know must have slipped my mind. I'm sure she did tell me! I say nervously as I glare at Lottie and she shrugs.

"Are you about to fire me now?" I say slipping down from the counter like an oiled-up snake, except the oil in my case is sweat from panicking.

"I think it's rather mandatory for the client to have an opinion on their boss but I didn't think this opinion would be so unorthodox." Nate says as I laugh a-little.

"Unironically all my opinions are unorthodox." I say as Lottie laughs.

"Well, Nesryn I hope to change your opinion the longer you work here." Nate says walking off Upstairs.

"Oh, Nesryn just fuck me already! "Lottie says smirking a wide smirk as I hit her shoulder.

"Shut up dude!" I hiss as Nate runs down the stairs in a pair of work out shorts and a workout vest. And Lottie's eyes instantly dart to him and I glare at her.

"I'm heading to the gym then back to work see you girls later!" Nate says as we wave Lottie Waves for the simple fact that for the first time in her life, she's speechless.

A couple hours later

I hear the preacher say
"Speak now or forever hold your peace"
There's a silence, there's my last chance
I stand up with shaking hands
All eyes on me
Horrified looks from everyone in the room
But I'm only look-in' at you
I am not the kind of girl
Who should be rudely barging' in on a white veil occasion
But you are not the kind of boy,
Who should be marrying' the wrong girl
So don't say yes, run away now
I'll meet you when you're out
Of the church at the back door

Don't wait or say a single vow
You need to hear me out
And they said, "speak now"
And you say, "let's run away now
I'll meet you when I'm out of my tux at the
back door
Oh baby, I didn't say my vow
So glad you were around when they said,
"speak now" we sing and she looks at me.

"Maybe he will sleep with you if you sing to
him!" She says looking at me.

"Oh, as if he would and I told you I don't sing
in front of people." I say as she frowns at me.

"So, what am I a seahorse?" She says looking
at me confused as I giggle.

"No, you are my cousin your family!" I say
laughing.

"Yeah, yeah whatever." She says giggling.

# CHAPTER TEN

And that was the first night I dreamt of Nate and me in many different positions each more captivating than the last. I've never dreamt like this before but the second my head hits the pillow a magical sexy scenario creeps into my subconscious state.

I am not a crude in fact one might call me a prude a Modern-day puritan a virgin a pure innocent beauty, if I must say so myself but the dreams I'm having are anything but pure or innocent.

I dreamt about him throwing me on the bed stripping me of my silk purple dress kissing down my neck leaving his mark on my body that' rough I'd feel it days after.

I dreamt that he'd walk in on me showering and look at me for a second before removing every layer of clothing he was wearing and grabbing the bottle of shower gel rubbing it up and down my body getting lower and lower each time.

I dreamt about riding him on his leather black sofa. In pure pleasure, I moan softly in his ear and lean my head back as he became harder and more intense underneath me. He'd flip me over and as he was about to enter me.

I awake to the horrible disappointment that he's my boss and I'm still a virgin.

I sit up in my bed sighing feeling my head as small beads of sweat drip from me.

Lottie comes slipping through the small space I leave open in my bedroom door and she just smirks at me.

"I'm a pretty little virgin!" She says twirling her hair mocking me as I roll my eyes.

"Ugh oh ugh fuck my harder Nate fuck ugh!" She says mocking me laughing as I get out of bed chasing her down the stairs as I almost stumbled on the last step.

"Girls, what the hell is going on!" Nan says crossing her arms. She looks at us confused as Lottie laughs behind Nan's back.

"Oh, nothing, she just took one of my tops and said it looks better on her it clearly doesn't." I say laughing as Lottie fake laughs loudly.

"Well, you better get ready for work or you're going to be late!" Nan says sternly looking at me and Lottie.

"You know what, I actually feel this little tickle on my throat. A little "cough cough." I say as Nan raises an eyebrow at me.

"Oh yeah, geez it sounds terrible." Lottie says sniggering at me. I stick my middle finger up at her when Nan's not looking.

"Well, you best go back to bed, I will bring up some of my homemade fish bone soup." Nan says smiling as Lottie makes a sickie face and I frown.

"You know, it's funny that Nan I'm actually suddenly feeling so much better!" I say smiling trying not to choke as Lottie makes funny faces behind Nan's back.

"Then what the hell are you girls doing chatting and wasting time? Go get dressed "she snaps as I run up the stairs to get ready.

"I take it your plan to avoid mister hotshot hasn't worked, trust me it's better this way nans fish soup is the worst!" Lottie says driving to work as I nod in agreement.

"How am I supposed to look at him when all I'm dreaming about is him? Ya know hot and sweaty with me?" I say going red looking at Lottie as she giggles.

"You know my first couple of days working there I dreamt about him too. It was so weird like he was in my thoughts!" Lottie says laughing as I sigh with relief knowing I'm not the only one.

"I know right it's so strange. "I say feeling confused as she nods in agreement.

"So, when's it gets better?" I ask feeling hopeful.

"Um it doesn't, you just learn to live with it. At least you're getting screwed in another dimension little virgin." Lottie says mockingly as I roll my eyes.

"What's wrong with being a virgin and can we not talk about virgin territory?" I snap crossing my arms defensively, getting out the car as I glare at her.

"Nothing it's just, isn't it boring being you know a virgin?" Lottie says acting like the word virgin is a swear word. She gets out and locks her car door. I just stand in the parking lot glaring at her.

"Who's a virgin?" Someone says behind us as I turn around and jump flushing red. It's Nate standing at his front door.

'Ugh, my cat is, I mean she's called Virgin, which is short for Virginia' I say, smiling helplessly knowing I just blew it.

"Dumb name." He states turning around laughing and walking into the house as I hit Lottie's arm and she yelps. To my surprise he takes the lie and actually believes it.

"I was thinking of taking the kids to our ball pit today. You want to come along girls?" Nate asks as

"But, but what about your work?" I say unable to make eye contact with my boss who I happened to have steamy shower sex with in my sleep last night.

"I um I'm not sure, I was planning to sit and make paper chains with the kids." I say trying to do anything in my power to avoid spending more time with him.

He says as Lottie gets up to answer for me: "I don't work Saturdays, are you in?".

"Course we are!" She says smiling as I roll my eyes.

# CHAPTER ELEVEN

"Hey Ness! "Nate calls as I turn around and a plastic red ball comes flying towards my face.

"Hey!" I shout as I try to run up to him in the ball pit with Tate on my back.

We face plant into the bouncy balls as Tate starts giggling.

I watch as Nate jumps off the edge of the climbing frame. I clap as Tate copies me.

"Tell me that, that is so attractive oh my god!" Lottie says smirking and swooning as I look at him do a backflip into the ball pit.

"Maybe a little." I whisper as she giggles.

I sit next to Tate as Lottie holds Lo and we eat our lunch.

"So how does it feel knowing I ended sorry, annihilate you in the ball pit. "Nates says taking a bite out of his cheese sandwich. I roll my eyes at his sly attempt to frustrate.

"So, you hit me a couple times in the face, it doesn't mean you win!" I say getting competitive!

"Okay so round two if you think you can beat me!" He says smirking.

"I know I can!" I say crossing my arms.

"Well done!" He says sarcastically crossing his arms.

"Great!" I say glaring at him.

As I am about to say something rude my phone rings. I start to pull it out of my bag and answer it.

"Yes." I say down the phone knowing who it is.

"It's nice to hear from you too!" Mother says on the phone as I sigh and get up walking over to a quiet area.

"Look Nessy Bean, I need you to come back." She says down the phone. She only ever calls me Nessy Bean when she wants something.

"What no, I've got a job and a life here!" I snap.

"Yeah well, me and Edger have booked a cruise and we need you to have Tay." Mum says as I roll my eyes.

"No, I like it here, I have a job!" I snap getting louder.

"I have booked the flight it is not refundable, you are coming home Nesryn!" Mum shouts down the phone.

"Hey you could always just pop on the plane and see Nan yourself maybe that would change your mind!" I snap as I put the phone down and sigh.

"What's wrong?" Nate says walking over looking at me concerned.

"Oh, nothing just my mother. You know what parents can be like? I mean not parents Cos like you are a parent right but like not you, you know!" I say nervously as Lottie laughs at me getting anxious.

"Right." Nate says as I laugh.

"So, we should get back." Nate says as my phone rings and rings but I ignore it.

Nate picks up the phone off the table and answers it.

"Yes." He says down the phone as my eyes grow wide and I frown at him and give him evils.

"She's not leaving you're going to have to bring him here." He says down the phone as I go bright red and

"Bye for now!" He says putting the phone down as I walk over to him and snatch the phone out of his hand and walk off.

"What's wrong Nesryn!" He says following me as Lottie takes the kids to the car.

"Ness." He says pulling my arm so I face him

"You overstepped a line okay, a line you shouldn't cross!" I snap as he frowns at me.

"I helped you, now you get to see your mum and brother!" He snaps.

"I never wanted to in the first place Nate, you don't know the first thing about me and sure I judged you but that doesn't mean you can hop into my business!" I snap.

"Okay!" He says throwing his hands up in surrender.

"Okay?" I say questioning his vague answer confused as he frowns.

"Am I then to fire you?" He laughed, saying, "you were right, I overstepped, are you done?"

"Yes, Nate because everything's one big joke one big laugh aye buddy!" I say mocking his mannerisms.

"Hey, you have your coping mechanisms and I have mine!" He says laughing as I roll my eyes.

"And what yours is acting like a stoner twenty-four seven when you don't even smoke, oh my god do you hear me my life's Degrassi high!" I say as I rub my forehead feeling tired and defeated.

"Great so here's something, you can deal with mum since you invited her!" I say smirking at him.

"I'm your boss, not your father Nesryn!" He says crossing his arms as I go bright red. Now that the dreams have returned, I remember the very graphic dreams.

"Well, yeah obviously I know you're not my daddy.... dad I mean dad you aren't my dad but you invited her, you deal with her!" I snap as I'm about to insult him by calling him a dick face, I quickly stop myself remembering he is my boss!"

I laughed as he said, "Fine, she seems like a breeze anyway!".

"You got another thing coming dude!" I say laughing.

# CHAPTER TWELVE

"I honestly can't believe he agreed to doing this, he must be insane!" Lottie says laughing whilst folding Emma's clean washing. I sit on the kitchen counter whilst the kids sleep.

"Or simple short answer, he's just stupid!" I state pulling myself off the counter as I hear Nate sound the car horn indicating that he's ready to leave.

"Give me a hug before you leave, and remember don't sleep with him!" Lottie says winking as I roll my eyes.

"Oh, as if I ever would, this is strictly business, I pick my mother up with him we sleep in a hotel room before we pick her up then we take her home simple!" I say shrugging and acting like it's not a big deal as I walk out to Nate's care.

"And hey if it's not simple there's always the backup plan, I will just have to jump out the window!" I say giggling and getting into Nate's car.

"Great plan girly, you ring me from the hospital and let me know if any hot guys stitch up your broken body!" She shouts out to me as I turn back and laugh as Nate's car pulls up to the drive way and I wave.

I get in and he drives off.

"Are you sure Emma is cool with this? With Lottie watching the kids and cleaning it's a lot for her don't you think?" I question as he drives down the road and I sigh feeling like I'm doing something wrong.

"Yes Ness, she is perfectly fine with this, like you said your mother's my responsibility I must look after her, right?" He says sarcastically smirking at me.

"Sure!" I say rolling my eyes at his pathetic attempt at sarcasm.

"On the road again!" I sing loudly and nod my head feeling bored!

Nate's gaze burns a hole in my head when I turn the pages of my book and put my legs Criss-cross apple sauce on the seat. I sigh loudly and flick through the pages.

"What, why are you staring at me dude?" I say glaring up at Nate seeing his eyes flick from the road to me every other second.

"Do you have to always be so fidgety?" He says laughing a few times.

"Yes, now entertain me I'm bored as shit oh I mean I." I say remembering he's my boss.

"You can swear Ness I'm not your owner look fuck, bastard, dick, bitch!" He says sounding like a proud child who's just been told they are allowed to swear for the first time. I clap and laugh like a seal.

"How long now until we get there?" I ask as I pull out my bottle of water and take a sip.

"Well approximately 3 hours and 35 minutes says the sat nav!" He says as I stare at him.

"Turn left at the next junction!" I say mocking the automated voice.

He smirks as he looks at me and says, "You're really funny.".

"I know right!" I say smirking like the Cheshire Cat.

Ten minutes later.

We need to stop and eat somewhere!" I groan, feeling my stomach growl.

"No but we can go to the McDonald's drive through!" He says and I smile getting my way.

Ten minutes

"You know Emma would absolutely kill me if she knew I was eating this, she wants me on an all-green diet!" He says laughing as he bites into his cheese burger and I giggle.

"Don't worry I'm not planning to rat you out, what Emma doesn't know won't hurt her right?" I say looking at him as he stares at me.

"Right!" He says almost like he's unsure if that's right but then he continues to drive.

"Sing with me!" I say laughing.

"You go talk to your friends my friends talk to me, weeeee are never getting back together!" I sing loudly as he taps his fingers on the wheel.

"So, he calls me up and he's like, "I still love
you"
And I'm like, "I just- I mean, this is
exhausting, you know?
Like, we are never getting back together, like,
ever" I say in a forced American accent and
he laughs at me

"I didn't know you could sing like that!" He
says raising his eyebrow at me.

"Like what aha!" I say laughing.

"You know do the high notes" he says
laughing.

"Well, they are actually easy try some!" I say
as he sings along and I hold my ears and
squill like a pig.

"Ugh I um I think you need a lot of umm
practice!" I say laughing trying to spare him
his feelings.

"Girl you know I just hit that note!" He says clicking his fingers like a diva.

"Hell yeah, you did!" I say nodding and giggling.

After a while I feel myself drifting off.

I am awoken by the raging sound of the car horn as I jump out of my sleep abruptly.

"What the hell Nate!" I say rubbing my eyes tiredly.

"We are at the hotel" He announces and I turn away from him.

"It's fine I will sleep right here." I say crossing my arms over me and hugging myself for warmth.

"No, you will sleep in the hotel room which I have just walked in and paid for all while you slept. Get out!" He says crossing his arms as he slams his door shut and walks over to my side.

"Fine okay, okay I'm coming!" I say getting out of the car shivering.

"This place, it's so fancy!" I say looking around the large room.

"They only had sales on couple specials for Valentine's Day so I figured I'd save some money." He says as I look around at the rose petals spread out on the bed and the champagne beside the bed along with red satin sheets.

"It's so cold." I say hugging myself for warmth. The only thing I brought was my I heart London hoodie.

"Here." He says slinging some joggers and a sweatshirt at me.

"Thanks." I say smiling half heartedly.

I walk into the bathroom and put the clothes on tying the sweatpants with a hair bobble at the waist so they fit. I walk over to the sink and wash my face I notice a small red heart bowl of condoms and a note saying be safe and sexy, eww.

I walk out and sit on the bed as Nate walks into the bathroom. I wonder if he notices the discreet protection package.

"I'm going to sleep on the floor. "Nate announces coughing awkwardly as he walks out the bathroom in his boxers and t shirts.

"I actually hate sleeping alone in hotel rooms anyways, please I promise I won't dribble on you. I can't say anything about snoring though." I say looking at him as he chuckles.

"Okay" he says as I see him crack a smile.

I climb into the bed feeling the comfortable satin sheets rub against my legs like a warm hug. Nate slides in away from me as far as possible and I lay on my back looking up at the ceiling fan spinning round and round making creaks with every movement it makes.

My hand is aware of something touching it. I feel his hand lock with mine and he strokes his fingers across the back of my hand. I feel a warmth flow to my cheeks.

I shut my eyes feeling complete and comfortable as I drift off to sleep.

Tomorrow, here we come, it's a big day.

# CHAPTER THIRTEEN

"Your mother's flight was supposed to land an hour ago, Nesryn she's not here!" Nate says tapping his foot impatiently as I roll my eyes and shake my head.

"No trust me, mum would be here okay it's not like her to just leave things she was going to drop Tay off, she needed me to babysit she needed something off me, she wouldn't just leave it, she wouldn't leave me!" I snap glaring at him as I sit in the seat anxiously as I look at the door and it opens.

"What the hell, hey!" I shout as I run up to Isabella noticing Tay in her arms.

"I missed you Nes Nes!" Tay says in baby talk whilst hugging me.

"It's okay baby, I'm not going anywhere, you are staying with me!" I say to Tay holding his face as Nate walks over and coughs awkwardly. He puts his hand on my lower back and I feel a spark fly through my stomach. I stand there feeling awkward.

"Right okay, umm Bella this is Nate, my boss. I'm the nanny for him and his wife. I look after his wonderful kids." I announce smiling at her as she looks at us suspiciously.

"Hello, Nate. Is it?" Bells asks waving a little at him as I place my hand on my forehead while feeling awkward.

"So, why's mother not coming this time and please don't tell me she paid...." I start to question as she holds up a fifty pound note up.

"Ouch, she'd rather pay you than risk having to spend a week with us, a week with me." I murmur as I hold Tay in my arms.

"So how long did she say I got Tay for?" I question as Bells gets Tays and her suitcase off the spiny thing.

"I'm not sure, she said she doesn't need you now that she has me to watch Tay as long as we are all out of her hair, she doesn't care what we do!" Bells says shrugging as I feel my heart sink.

I walk over to the car feeling tired. I get in the front and sit next to Nate quietly.

Is everything okay, did you guys figure it out?" He asks with a sincere smile.

"I wish." I say as I sink deeper into the leather seat.

Ten minutes later and the car is silent until Nate decides to kill the silence.

"Hey little man, why don't we get you some pizza for dinner?" Nate asks Taylor as Tay nods happily.

"We are here you guys wait in the car while I get the pizza." Nate says smiling at me.

"Me come, me come!" Tay says as I smile at Nate innocently.

"Okay come on then little man!" Nate says picking up Taylor from his car seat in the back of the car.

"So how long are you here b?" I question smiling at her as Nate walks off with Tay in his arms.

In a week, me and Taylor will ship back to my dad's, and my dad agreed to watch him with me!" Bella sighs and I nod.

I wish my dad was around.

"I got so much to show you, here is so different to back home, it's crazy!" I announce smiling whilst looking back at her in the backseat.

"Oh my god, you are totally crushing on him I can tell, look at that glow!" She squeals as I go red.

"Is it that obviously? " I ask, blushing bright red.

"He's so, so, so into you!" She says smugly like she knew it before I did.

"Nothing could ever happen; he's married, happily married he's from a whole different rich universe to me!" I say as she laughs at me.

"What?" I ask suddenly becoming self-conscious, crossing my arms.

"You have just grown up so much, you know back home you would've hooked up with him just to piss mum off!" Bells says as I giggle and nod in agreement.

"I don't know, I guess for the first time ever it just feels like I'm home and I don't want to screw anything up!" I say laughing as we hear guys laughing outside the car. I turn to the left to see two teenage boys standing looking at me and bells as I raise my left eyebrow slightly, confused as to why they are looking at us.

Bella instantly smirks widely and climbs out the backseat of the car, pulling down her skirt that she's wearing and adjusting her Victoria Secret pink T-shirt to show a little more cleavage. She starts to make her way over to them like a cheetah slow and ready to devour their pry, I sigh and make my way out the car following slowly her.

# CHAPTER FOURTEEN

"Hey so do you wanna go out sometime? Could I maybe get your number, It'd be chill !" The boy with ginger messy hair nonchalantly says to Bells as I stand behind her observing her flirty behaviour taking notes, the way she's twiddling her long ash blonde hair but not too much to the point he'd notice but just enough to make her hair look wind swept.

The way she knew he was going to ask for her number because all the guys do. However, she still acted ever so surprised like she'd never had a guy ask for her number before in her life, I mean like I haven't.

"Yeah sure, here!" She says shrugging like it's no big deal but inside I know she's internally freaking out with euphoria. She gets out her phone from her small black handbag that hangs off her shoulder messily. I stand there feeling stupid whilst the ginger haired boys friend sits on the bench smoking a cigarette behind us.

I walk over to him and sit on the top of the bench with my knees up.

"Wow that's so cool dude!" I say sarcastically as he smirks.

"It's not supposed to be, do you want one?" He says as I raise my eyebrow.

"What am I supposed to do with it? Shove it up my ass, Nah I'm good you keep the cancer stick thanks!" I say playfully as he rolls his green eyes and starts to scribble something on a piece of paper.

"Oh so you are one of those!" He says as I giggle and nod.

"Yep." I say grinning.

"I'm Luke" he says extending a hand for me to shake.

"I'm Nes I mean Nesryn, my name is Nesryn!" I say nervously taking his hand in mine and shaking it.

"Rad name see you round Nesryn!" He states getting up off the bench and on his skateboard, skating off.

I look on the bench and see the scrap piece of paper that he wrote on. I open it and it says.

"Hey here's my number if you can handle the cig smell." :)"

I run up to Bella jumping up and down as she starts to jump with me.

"I just got his number B!" I say smiling.

"He was so cute, you lil baller!" Bells says getting back into the car.

"What'd we miss?" Nate questions walking to the car with two boxes of pizza piled up on top of each other and carrying Tay in his free hand.

"Nothing much just Nesryn scoring a hot guys number!" Bells chimes whilst smirking.

"That's great Nes, you're getting yourself out there more!" He says smiling whilst looking at the road as I grit my teeth feeling awkward.

"Come on let's get you guys home!" Nate says calmly but I sense a hint of defensiveness in his tone.

"Okay." I whisper looking at him.

The drive home is silent, long and awkward to say the least.

We all get out the car and Nan is fast asleep in bed so I tell them to be quiet as Bells carries Taylor in since he's asleep.

"Here let me help with them!" Nate says taking two of the suitcases.

"Thank you for everything, the job, for today." I say smiling as I feel my heart sink.

"it's no biggy," he says smiling at me.

"I really needed my mum to come today, to care." I say as my smile falls flat.

He looks at me sympathetically.

"Please don't, don't do that, don't look at me like I'm a fragile little girl who just needs comfort. I just thought for the first time in a while my mother would care about me like mothers do but I was wrong. I am always wrong."I mumble as tears start to fall from my eyes uncontrollably.

It's strange but when I'm around him I feel a sense of freedom. I could say anything, say anything offensive even and he wouldn't care and he wouldn't judge. He'd just listen.

"I was stupid!" I say laughing bitterly as I wipe my eyes.

"Nes, you don't need her, you have other people you have me." He says holding my hand as I look up at him.

And it falls silent.

"Did you know my older brother is in prison? He used to abuse me, he'd hit me and mentally torture me but it didn't matter how he'd treat me, I'd forgive him no matter what." I say as I feel more tears brimming.

"He was my only full sibling, and he was supposed to protect me but he blamed me, for dad, for everything." I say as I look up at Nate.

"I'm so sorry Nesryn." He says embracing me in a warm hug as I smell his sweet vanilla and dark berry cologne.

"I'm not strong I act so hard and tough I'm not, I'm scared!" I say crying as he hugs me.

I look up at him and then feel a flush of embarrassment fill me.

I look down digging my face into his dark brown sweater.

"I'm so hopeless!" I say laughing helplessly.

"No you're not, your just different. I've never met anyone like you before!" He states as I feel his eyes on me and I look down at the floor going shy again.

"Really? " I say smiling up at him trying to regain composure.

"Really." He says looking into my eyes as his hand makes its way to my jaw. I hear my Nan's bedroom door open.

"Anyways, it's getting late you should umm you should get home you're probably so tired." I say stuttering knowing I don't want him to go but he has to. I feel sorrow at the thought of him leaving. I wipe my eyes with the arm of my sweatshirt.

"Yeah I probably should. I will see you tomorrow Nesryn." He says smiling at me.

"Thanks, again" I shout to him as he looks back and smiles.

I shut the door and walk to the kitchen. I sit at the table and just think about letting silence surround me.

# CHAPTER FIFTEEN

"Oh my god, you actually cried in front of him, you haven't even cried in front of me yet!" Lottie says sitting at the bottom of my bed while Tay lays inbetween me and bells.

"Yep when I came downstairs Nes was sat at the table crying whilst eating chocolate chip cookies!" Bella says laughing, as I go red with embarrassment.

"Honestly where have you been all my whole life?" Lottie says to Bells and I laugh.

"With this tearful queen!" Bells says smiling at me.

"How are you feeling, are you excited?" Bells says smiling.

Feeling confused, I ask, "No excited about what, should I be?".

"Well yeah, it's your birthday tomorrow, duh!" Bells says as Lottie claps her hands excitedly.

"Oh, I completely forgot it must of slipped my mind, it's because I've been so busy with mum's shit lately!" I say as Bella laughs.

"We gotta party, we have to get drunk!" Lottie says smiling

"No way, I've turned over a new leaf in my life and rule one is no drinking, anyways I hate getting drunk!" I say smiling as bells and Lottie's faces fall flat.

"Oh, come on, just because mother turns into an alcoholic every time husband number whatever leaves her doesn't mean you have to stop yourself from having fun and being a fun sucker!" Bells says as I roll my eyes.

Lottie says, "Wow, way harsh, Bells!".

"No, she's right I denied myself fun way too many times, but it won't happen any longer. I still won't be drinking!" I say smiling at bells and sticking my middle finger up at her.

"How exciting because those cute boys invited us to a party next week and we are going!" Bells says as Lottie laughs and raises her eyebrow intrigued by what she hears.

"Yes you too were invited in fact they have a single mate who just came out of an abusive toxic relationship!" Bells says smirking as I roll my eyes.

"Just my type!" Lottie states and Bells giggles.

It's like they are both just staring in the mirror at themselves. They instantly hit it off which is exactly what I planned for!

It's strange but I'm nervous to see Luke again. The only time I've ever liked a guy was when I fell in love with them, and that never ends well; let's list them.

Blue, my first ever real love, was my best friend growing up. When the girls would push me about in school he'd push them back. He'd always ring me talking to me for hours. I'd tell him about my brother hurting me and calling me fat and telling me to kill myself. He'd ask if I wanted him to beat him up for me. I'd always say no because I knew he'd get floored but it was still a thoughtful gesture.

I'd pretend that I cared about all the girls he dated and would be so invested and then they'd be together and I'd feel so jealous. Then they'd break up and I'd be his number one again, that is until I left school. I never saw him again after that.

Then came Cas My middle school best friend Dani's friend. He used to be a dick to me but it made me like him so much more. I wanted no, I needed him to have a secret soft spot for me. I wanted an enemies to lovers romance with him. It's safe to say that was the year I discovered Wattpad.

Long story short he was a dick to me because he actually did hate me and when I went to kiss him he was repulsed.

Then Spencer my sweet Spencer I was 12 and I was being bullied by the popular girls and had no one to hang out with. He'd follow me around school and we'd sit together at computer time we'd share headphones and listen to red by Taylor Swift it was good times but back then dating me was seen as gross since I was considered as fat and ugly so he didn't date me but we were good Friends, and I always wondered what it would've been like if we were more I knew deep down he did as-well as , we'd walk the dogs together in the snow and he'd always walk me home and hug me goodbye.

Some times I wonder if Spencer has forgotten about me.

I haven't forgotten about him, I could never do so.

Anyway those loves of mine have flown to the stars and clouds.

It just doesn't feel realistic having a romance right now with looking after Tay and work and mum's manic life I don't see how it'd work out .

# CHAPTER SIXTEEN

"Happy birthday cutie." I read the message to myself that Luke had just sent me as I smiled to myself.

"Morning, happy birthday!" Tay shouts running into my bedroom with Lottie and Bella by his side.

"Thank you, guys!" I say smiling widely.

"Morning sweetie," Nan says knocking on my bedroom door before walking in my room.

"Morning Nan!" I say hugging her as she hides her right hand behind her back.

She leans back. She holds out a gift box out in front of me as I look at it confused.

"You didn't have to; you know I hate gifts." I say as she nods.

"I didn't, your father asked me to give it to you before he died." She says as Bells and Lottie look at me and my cheeks go bright red and I can feel tears ready to brim in my eyes at the sound of the words "your father".

I open the box and inside is a beautiful gold ring with purple crystals in the middle.

There's a note.

I open it.

To my sweet baby Nesryn finally nineteen one year left until you're out of your teen years please enjoy it mum gave me this ring to propose to your mother but when your mother declined my offer, I knew it had to go to you I have eternal love for you that will never fade even when I'm not around, please enjoy your life and live to the fullest my darling Nesryn.

Love you, dad.

Tears flow down my eyes as I fold the note and tuck it into my journal that's beside my bed.

"It's beautiful." I say looking intently at the vintage looking gold ring.

"It's what my grandad proposed to my Nan with and then my dad to my mum then my husband to me and your father to your mother and now to you." Nan says smiling as I hug her.

"Thank you, I mean it's amazing." I say hugging her and wiping away my tear.

"Go get ready, you and Lottie are going to be late for work. Me and Joyce have Tay, right?" Bells says looking at Nan.

"Yeah." Nan says smiling.

Bella calls Nan Joyce because she's not Bella's Nan and it makes Bella's dad mad.

I get dressed into a red long sleeve ribbed top and high waisted black ripped jeans and my red converse.

Lottie convinces me to put some mascara blush and lip gloss on since it's my birthday.

TWENTY MINUTES LATER

I walk into the house with Lottie I notice Emma's sat with the kids in the kitchen as I shrug off my jacket and put it on the coat rail.

Nate is standing with his back to us cooking scrambled eggs wearing black jogger shorts and a loose green sports t shirt.

"Lottie, would you mind making the beds?" Emma says smiling at her.

"I will do that now for you!" Lottie says smiling whilst putting her jacket and shoes down and walking upstairs.

"Nes, would you mind taking over feeding lo, I am late for work?" Emma asks standing up.

I smile as I reply, "Of course." She kisses Nate and leaves.

"Hey Nate." I say smiling as he turns round to face me.

"So, birthday girl do you want some eggs?" He says smirking as I put my hands over my eyes.

"Oh no Lottie told you, I was trying to keep it low-key:" I say as he chuckles and I go red.

"I can do low-key; I can so do low-key!" He says shrugging.

"Happy birthday Nes Nes Nes!" Logan and Tate shout as I stand up and hug Logan and Tate.

"Thank you, cuties." I say as I notice Nate looking at me intensely.

"Oh no, do I look that ridiculous! I told Bells not to curl my hair but she didn't listen!" I say sighing as he smiles softly at me.

"You look good Nes." He says smiling at me as I feel my cheeks flush.

"Nes, we're tired." Tate says as I smile and pick Logan up and hold Tate's hand. I walk them upstairs to the bedroom. I tuck them into bed.

"Lay with us." Tate says as I lay down with them and Logan giggles.

"Story story." He says smiling.

"Okay, one day there was this girl stuck with an evil curse from the evil witch named June and her crazy wizard called Edger. She escaped the castle and ran away but no one could see how beautiful she was not even herself because of the curse then she runs into the magic prince with his beautiful blue eyes. They fall in love and he kisses her and breaks the curse but then the big evil fart monster tries to fart on her head pop pop pop and she blows away." I say giggling as Logan and Tate laugh.

I sit there as they start to fall asleep and my eyes get heavy.

And I fall asleep too.

# CHAPTER SEVENTEEN

"Nes, Nesryn, Nes." I hear Someone say as they shake me awake.

As I sit up, I realize I've fallen asleep.

"Oh my god Nate, I'm so sorry this is so unprofessional, Oh Shit!" I mumble feeling stressed out.

"Hey, it's fine Lottie took the kids to get ice cream. She said you looked too peaceful to wake." He says smiling at me.

"She did?" I ask confused, what in the world is she playing at, what's her game?

"Yeah. "He says chuckling lowly.

"Oh, what a gem." I say sighing with relief but also knowing what she's thinking.

"Oh, I got to get up, its nearly six and I need to get ready for tonight." I say getting up off of Tate's bed.

"For tonight?" he questions, his eyebrow raised slightly.

"Luke asked me out.. I was supposed to go home early and Lottie was supposed to cover me so Bells could teach me how to slow dance." I say pacing back and forth.

"I screwed up being lazy and sleeping!" I say as Nate reaches out and touches my arm. My hand moves back slightly as I feel myself jolted.

"I can help, I know a thing or two about dancing." He says smirking as I giggle.

"You do? I mean yeah sure, Okay." I say smiling.

"Meet me in the front room in ten minutes bring your phone." He says laughing.

"Okay." I say smiling as he walks out of the room.

Ten minutes later I walk down the stairs with my phone in my hand feeling small. Nate is sat on the sofa twiddling with his hands nervously. He stands up when he sees me.

"Pick a song and plug it into the speaker." He says standing up, and smiling.

"Oh, this is embarrassing." I say, hiding my face as he chuckles.

"What's wrong?" He asks.

"The only songs I have downloaded are from what my dad used to play when I was a kid.

He loved old music." I say turning red and he smiles.

" Pick any, I promise I won't laugh." He states smiling as I feel my cheeks heat up.

I plug my phone into the speaker and click shuffle on my phone.

Autumn in New York by Jo Stafford starts to play.

"Are you okay?" Nate says looking at me as I listen to the start of the song letting the memory of my father telling me how he met my mother flood my ears.

"Yeah, this was the song playing when my dad first met my mum. They met in a quaint French cafe a few blocks away from our home she had an angel face my father said, and when they bumped into each other they both looked up at the same time and they knew it was love. "I say feeling the pit in my stomach rising.

"Well, from my father's perspective it was love." I say looking down.

Nate pulls me close to him and I feel his hands snake around my waist and my breath hitches.

"Put your arms around my neck." He says and I do it and we start to two step back and forth.

Nate's hand travels down my back, he leans me down letting my hair fall freely.

He lifts me up and the song comes to an end. I'm sweating, I'm not sure if it's because I'm out of breath or because his hands are on my body.

"Thanks." I say looking up at him, he looks down at me and smiles.

"You are welcome." He mumbles still holding me in his arms.

I hear the front door open and I step back from him and unplug my phone.

"We are back" Lottie says smiling looking at me ominously. I roll my eyes.

"It's getting dark, I should be getting back home I just need to call a taxi." I say smiling at Lottie.

"I can take you if Lottie doesn't mind watching the kids." Nate offers.

"You really don't have...." I start to say as Lottie interrupts.

"That's so considerate of you Nate, of course I will!" Lottie says smirking at me.

"Thanks." I say smiling weakly.

"It's no problem." Nate says smiling as I walk out to his car and he follows me.

We sit in silence as he drives me home.

As he parks on a quiet street, I ask confused, "What are you doing?".

He turns on the car light and looks at me.

"I got you something." He says fiddling with his hidden compartment by the steering wheel, he pulls out a small box.

"You didn't have to. " I say as I blush.

"I wanted to. "He mumbles nervously.

I open the box and it's a charm bracelet with a little microphone on it.

"The other day when you sang it was brilliant, I will forever remember you as the girl who sings like an angel." Nate says smirking.

"I don't know what to say, it's perfect." I say looking at him as he smiles.

I undo my seat belt and lean over to him hugging him and smelling his vanilla and cherry cologne.

I lean back into my seat looking at him as he leans his head forward looking at me as my phone vibrates.

I lean back in my seat and check my phone.

It's bells.

"That's my sister, she's probably wondering where I am. I can walk the rest of the way it's only like one street over." I say smiling.

"Okay." He says looking at me.

"See you tomorrow, Nate." I say shutting the car door as he doesn't say anything.

# CHAPTER EIGHTEEN

I am sat waiting outside the restaurant waiting for Luke as the time keeps ticking.

About an hour passes by and I'm sitting on the curb with tears in my eyes. I messaged Lottie telling her and she said Nan wouldn't let her out the house so I'm just waiting for the bus. Nate's car pulls up and he rolls the window down as I stand up.

"Lottie called and said you needed me" he says as I smile half-heartedly.

"I do thank you." I say as I open the door and get out the car.

"Is Emma okay with this?" I ask as he looks at me.

"She's away for a couple of days, on a work trip. "He says playing with the heating settings on the car dashboard.

"I thought he liked me. I really thought he liked me. How fucking stupid of me!" I say sighing bitterly as he stops the car.

"You aren't stupid." He says gruffly, whilst looking at me.

"I got all dressed up because Bella and Lottie said he wouldn't like me dressed how I was, what a waste." I say sighing.

"You look gorgeous Nesryn." He says holding my chin up as I look at him.

"You really think so?" I say looking at him confused.

"I really do." He says as I look at him and unbuckle my seat belt quickly leaning forward as I look in his eyes and he does that smirk that he does.

He grips my thigh and I gasp; he opens his mouth and his smirk gets wider; he pulls me onto his lap abruptly.

I lean in close to him as I run my hands through his mousy brown hair.

He gripped my waist with his hand.

"I don't think we should be doing this Nate." I whisper as he leans his head back sighing in frustration.

"You're right." He mumbles as I get off his lap and sit back in my seat.

The rest of the ride is quiet until I get out at my house, he says.

"Happy birthday Nesryn." He says smiling.

"Thank you, Nate." I smiled and shut the car door and ran up the steps to my house holding my skirt down from the wind.

"Holy shit oh my god!" I say as I shut the front door behind me. The house is pitch black and then the lights turn on bells and Lottie are standing in front of me.

"Where were you young lady?" Lottie says tapping her feet like a mother as I jump at her and bells.

"Omg I nearly kissed him!" I say as Bella begins to scream and me and Lottie hold her mouth.

"Oh my god Luke nearly kissed you!" Lottie says as I roll my eyes.

"No about that he ditched me, Lottie remembers I texted you and you texted Nate." I say looking at Nate as she smirks.

"Oh, my you nearly kissed Nate!" Lottie says jumping up and down.

"I could feel the sexual tension with you two the other day ah, I'm so happy!" Bells says as I glare at her.

I say as they giggle, "I'm not looking forward to that awkward encounter with him on Monday."

"Come on go to bed now you big slut!" Lottie says smacking my butt as I walk upstairs and she giggles.

That night I dreamt about what would've happened if we did kiss.

# CHAPTER NINETEEN

The summer beach party Emma throws every year is in full swing and I'm watching and playing with Tate and Logan while Lottie hands out mini foods.

Nate is standing next to his boxer mates as they all stand like statues with beers in their hands making awkward small talk. Meanwhile, the other rich women sit on the garden sofa and gossip with Emma.

"Who's this small rocket?" Someone says from behind me as I turn and look up.

"Excuse me?" I say glaring at the guy with ginger hair and a cringey grin on his face.

"Come on babe, let's go for a dip." He says as I scowl and pull my hand out of his grip.

"Thanks, but not going to happen!" I hiss as I turn away and I feel myself being lifted bridle style.

"Get off me, get off me now!" I shout swatting at his hands violently.

"Tony stop!" Nate shouts his voice becoming deep and intimidating as Emma sits and laughs bubbly.

"Get off me please!" I beg as he throws me into the pool. My whole-body soaks in water as I shut my eyes.

Then I'm brought up to the surface.

I saw everyone laughing even Emma giggling and I ran into the house as fast as my legs could carry me.

I ran up to the bathroom and walked in shutting the
Door, I put my head in my hands as I hear a knock.

"Nes". I hear Nate calling as I ignore him.

Without warning he walks in and shuts the door.

"Tony's a dick, he was back in high school" He states as he leans down next to me with a towel in his hand as I sit on the floor and he takes a seat.

"I'm all gross and wet, my mascara is running everywhere, he completely embarrassed me, what an asshole." I mumble as Nate smiles.

"You're the only one I like here and the little ones and Lottie." I say being honest.

"About the other night" he starts to say as I cut him off.

"It was totally my fault I was being forward and inappropriate." I say as he chuckles.

"Trust me it wasn't one sided." He says, his eyes becoming dark and cloudy as I look at him intently.

"It wasn't?" I question, feeling confused.

"No, I wanted it as much as you did." He says and then looks down like a shy teenage boy with a crush as I smile.

"I want it, I really do." I whisper as he looks up at me.

"Me too." He says putting his hand on top of mine. I look at him and raise my eyebrow.

I feel his hand move and hold my waist. He lifts me onto his lap as I feel him underneath me.

I gasp and run my hand through his messy hair. He leans in and touches my lips softly with his. He pulls me up because I'm slipping down him as his t shirt gets wet from my soaked clothes.

"Kiss me, please, please just kiss me." He mutters as I nod and do as he says and the kiss deepens

When I pull away and look away he pulls my chin back up with his finger and attaches his lips to mine as he moves faster. I feel his tongue pushing my lips apart and I let it, I open my mouth and his hands go up my back touching my bare skin as he explores every angle of my mouth with his tongue, and I feel like I'm in a fairy-tale.

I pull at his hair as he kisses down my neck. I slowly start to grind my hips against him as he groans deeply.

I pull away quickly.

"I shouldn't have done that." I say trying to catch my breath as I touch my lips feeling a sad absence from his warm lips. He looks at me hungry for more.

I stand up and prepare to walk out but he grabs my hand and pulls me back as he shuts the door and pushes me against it. He kisses me more intensely as I moan against his lips and he bites my bottom lip.

"I shouldn't have done that now we are even."
He says smirking as I stand there my mouth
wide open in shock.

"I need a T shirt." I say quietly as he walks
into
His bedroom, I follow behind him feeling
unstable.

"I want to go back home can you take me?" I
ask as I reach out and touch his hand.

"Yeah, just let me clear it with Lottie, Emma's
drunk anyway she won't care." He says as he
hands me a long sleeve football t shirt.

I turn away from him as he walks out of the
bedroom. I lift my wet top off I put his one on
and then pull my wet leggings off because his
top is like a dress on me.

I take my hair out of its ponytail letting it
flow off of my shoulders.

"Ready." He says walking up to me holding the small of my back as I jump a little startled.

# CHAPTER TWENTY

And that was it for the next two weeks. I'd spend time with the kids and Lottie sometimes Emma but never Nate. He was away on a work trip of some sort. However, I couldn't help the pit in my stomach and the feeling that maybe it's my fault after what happened at the summer party.

It's Saturday night, me Lottie and the kids are sitting on the sofa watching the Lorax when the front door opens. I don't look up because I expect Emma to be home around this time.

"Daddy, daddy! "Tate calls jumping off the sofa and running up to the door. I turn to see Nate standing in the door way in grey suit trousers and a white shirt and grey tie.

What could he do with that tie, aye?

SHUT UP SUBCONSCIOUS.

"Hey." Nate mumbles not making eye contact with me after he says hi to Lottie.

"Hi." I answer bluntly, not sure how to talk to him. Things feel different, icy.

"Lottie stay here with Nate whilst I get the kids to bed." I order as she smirks.

"Oh, no you have a headache let me, you stay chat to Nate!" she says as I glare at her warningly.

"No!" I snap Firmly as she jumps a bit, as do the children.

"I mean, it's the job I get paid for it wouldn't be very professional of me if I sat here and chatted all day." I announce holding Tate's hand in one of my hands and Lo in my other arm.

No that wouldn't be very professional of me but making out with my boss wasn't very professional of me yet I still went and did it.

I hear Lottie mumble something about sexy, dream and boss and I shoot a warning glare her way and she shuts up.

After getting the kids to sleep I walk downstairs into the kitchen but Lottie isn't there no more.

"Where's Lottie?" I question looking at Nate.

"I told her to go to the shop to get the kids some cookies for the morning. When she gets back, I said I'd drop you home." Nate speaks as I glare at him.

"Why would you do that? I can find my own way home, Lottie was my ride home!" I snap crossing my arms becoming defensive.

"Did I do something, Nesryn?" Nate questions as I huff out, as if he doesn't know?

"You left after nearly...." I start to say as I stop myself realising what I'm about to say.

"No, no you didn't do anything." I mumble, stopping in my tracks, almost making a tit of myself.

"Okay I'm glad that's sorted." He says smirking so I continue to glare at him.

Asshole.

"Yep." I say not making eye contact with him.

"How was the work trip?" I ask making small talk with him as he laughs.

"That, it wasn't a work trip I just wanted to speak to my lawyer." He says as I look at him.

"Your lawyer?" I question as he nods.

"About a divorce." He says as I look at him confused.

"I thought you two loved each other?" I ask feeling confused.

"We did, did being past tense, she cheated on me." He says as I nod.

That's why he's been so helpful and made me feel wanted he wanted me to be his minuscule bit of revenge.

Well, I won't.

"I need to leave!" I announce quietly walking out the kitchen as he follows me. He pulls my arm back as my body turns with it so that I'm facing him.

"Why are you being like this, why are you being so skittish, do I make you uncomfortable? "He questions as I nod. Obviously.

"Yeah, you do, everything about you makes me uncomfortable and that stupid nice act isn't working no more!" I snap my cheeks going red with anger.

"Is that so, Nesryn?" He questions sarcasm dripping from him as I grab my bag walking out to the garage.

"Yes, Nate that is so and you know what, I QUIT!" I snap getting up in his face. He pulls me into him abruptly kissing me hard. For a second, I feel like I'm not breathing. I'm pretty sure I'm not.

"Huh. "I mumble pulling away from the kiss looking up at him as he holds my neck pulling my lips back to his.

He abruptly pulls off my tartan green shirt and I run my hands through his hair as the kiss deepens. He lifts me up carrying me to the back of his car in the garage.

"Do you trust me not to hurt you?" He questions putting me down in the backseat. My eyes look up at his. "Yes." I said almost instantly regretting it.

He turns me around abruptly so I'm looking through the back window of the car.

I try to turn my head to look at him but he pushes my head back hard against the seat.

"Nate, what are you doing?" I question feeling confused.

"Shh, you trust me right." He says as I nod trying to calm my nerves.

He pulls off my jeans revealing my underwear and leaving my legs completely bare.

"Nate." I mumble feeling him against me.

"Umm." He hums as I push him back a little.

"You're hurting, why are you being so rough?" I question quietly as he leans back into the seat and I push myself up onto his lap.

"Sorry, it's been a while." He says as I smirk.

"I knew my assumption was correct." I smugly reply.

"Okay okay, smarty." He says leaning into me kissing my neck as I feel him grind deeply into me feeling him against my underwear.

"Ready." He says as I lift myself up off him and he puts on protection.

"I don't know... Nate we are outside and it's my first, I don't want.." I start to say as I stop and gasp feeling him grab onto me pulling me on his lap.

He pushes my underwear to the side, He pushes deep into me with the skilled rolling of his hips, stirring deep inside me.

A scream is ripped through my throat but he pushes his lips onto mine to silence me. He thrusts harder pulling my hair back aggressively at the same time.

He is tireless, relentless, screwing me long and hard until my dark thoughts lose and I cry violently. This seems to turn him on more because he lets out a deep groan and slows his roll.

"Fuck." He mumbles kissing my shoulder blade.

I get up removing him from me, I pull my underwear up and wipe my eyes.

"You're crying, what's wrong?" he asked, touching my thigh.

"Nothing, it was my first time it hurt that's all."
I mumble as he pulls me close to him.

"I'm sorry baby, next time will be better." He says as I lean into his shoulder.

"Could you take me home?" I ask as he shakes his head.

"I can't after what we just did, that'd look suspicious." He says as I pull my jeans back on.

"Right, well I will see you Monday I guess." I mumble getting out of the car.

"I thought you quit?" Nate questions on a serious note.

"Right yeah I quit." I mumble.

"See you soon?" I say almost questioningly.

"I'm not sure, maybe." He says quietly as I nod. I quickly slammed the car door and started to run.

I get in the house in a rush and run upstairs to my room where Bella is playing hot wheels with Tay on the floor.

"Nes, what's wrong why are you bleeding?" Bella says looking at my teary face.

"Nothing, I fell over on the way home." I say looking down at the blood stain on the crotch of my jeans.

# CHAPTER TWENTY ONE

The next day

I'm sat in the bath with my knees pulled up to my face when Bella walks in abruptly without knocking.

"Ness." Bell says as I don't look up and I continue to ignore her.

"Please talk to me I'm worried. I saw you take the pill this morning." Bell says as I just ignore her.

"What did you do Nesryn, please tell me, maybe I can help" she says as I break down into tears.

Without a word she gets into the bath fully clothed and cradles me, something she used to do when I was a child and mum would ignore me.

"Nesryn, are you okay?" Lottie says walking into the bathroom as I nod and hide my body behind the shower curtain, but I start to cry again.

"You slept with him, didn't you?" Lottie questions as I nod.

"It hurt so bad, it wasn't what I thought it'd be, he wasn't gentle." I mumble as Bella hugs onto me.

"Did you tell him it was your first time?" Bella asks as I nod.

"I tried to, but he was so eager." I mumble.

"Babes you just slept with a married man!" Bella announces as I glare at her.

"You think I don't know that, anyway he told me he's getting a divorce. "I say looking at her as she looks at Lottie and Lottie looks back at me.

"Come on get out the bath, we got work!" Lottie says abruptly as I look at her and shake my head.

"I can't, I quit." I mumble.

"Was that before or after you slept with him?" Bella questions as Lottie glares at her.

"'Not helping!" I state getting out of the bath wrapping the towel around me.

"Get ready we are going to work. You got to get your last wages anyway, Emma told me last night." Lottie says as I nod.

"But I slept with her husband!" I say almost like I am just now realising it.

"Well, it's too late to question what's morally right." Bella says as Lottie nods in agreement.

"I didn't want it to be like that you know, I thought he'd take it slow, I thought we'd just kiss." I mumble walking into my bedroom drying myself and pulling my underwear up and on.

"Just as long as Emma doesn't find out, things will be fine." Lottie says as I nod.


An hour later.


"Lottie I'm so scared!" I mumble feeling tears about to brim as Emma opens the front door.

"I've come to collect my last cheque." I start to say getting stopped by the abrupt motion of her cold Boney hand against my face.

"That's for fucking my husband." She shouts loudly as tears threaten to spill.

I look up whilst holding my cheek firmly seeing Nate staring at me guiltily.

"You are both fired." Emma says shoving two envelopes into Lottie's hand, then slamming the door in our face.

We are both walking down the road when Nate calls out my name.

"Could you wait in the car for me?" I ask and she nods.

I stop dead in my tracks waiting for him to catch up to me.

"You told me you were getting a divorce, you lied!" I say rage rushing through me, like a house fire spreading.

"Calm down Nesryn I inquired. Sure but it wasn't set in stone. Me and Emma have a lot to sort through but did you really think I would end my marriage for you, a teenager?" He says in such a condescending tone.

"I thought you..." I mumble as tears brim in my eyes.

"You thought what, Nesryn you are a kid you thought we'd run away together then do what, adulthood doesn't work like that, it's something your father should've taught you!" He shouts as a sob rips from my throat.

A second later I'm being dragged away from him hitting out and kicking like the child I am.

Lottie starts to drive away with me sat in the front seat my eyes streaming with soggy tears.

"Let me out." I mumble as Lottie looks at me, concern playing on her face.

"But Nesryn I'm worried about you." She says quietly.

"Just let me the fuck out and go home!" I hiss angrily as the car comes to an abrupt holt.

As soon as I get out of the car, I start running. I keep running until I feel my heart pounding out of my chest, is that even possible?

I wish dad was here.

I wish dad was.

I wish.

Dad.

Here.

"I'm ready to leave now." I shout looking down at the cliff in front of me.

"Let me go now god I'm ready!" I scream loudly.

I pull my bag off my shoulder and set it down on the ledge along with my phone and door keys to the house.

I pull my jacket off but leave my jeans and shirt on.

"What the fuck, Nesryn!" Nate says pulling me back from the edge of the cliff as I turn to him with all the will I have in me, I push him back.

"Don't stop me to save your shitty conscience." I hiss out, letting my cynical self flourish.

"You are acting crazy!" He says pulling my shoulder.

"I am being me, maybe I am fucking crazy but I know what's for certain, I am done." I mumble looking at the no cliff jumping sign.

And I go.

I do it too, but so does he.

He's stopping me, maybe he cares, maybe we both die.

Maybe we end up together somewhere else maybe this is his way of leaving with me and we meet in another life.

I shut my eyes feeling the sting of the cold water hit my body with a thud. I hit something sharp and everything blacks out.

# CHAPTER TWENTY TWO

Three weeks later.

"Grams I love you, please don't hate me." I mumble as tears shoot down my face. My Nan grabs my hand holding it in hers squeezing tightly like if she lets go I will disintegrate in front of her.

"I love you Nesryn, it's been nice having you stay. "She says kissing two fingers and placing them on the stitches on my left cheek.

"It was nice seeing you again Isabella. Tell your mother I said hi will you." Nan asks, whilst hugging Bella and high fiving Tay.

"Goodbye Nan." I mumble walking out the front door to Lottie's car where she waits to take us to the airport.

Nate told Nan and Lottie and Bell that I tripped and fell. He also said that he tried to save me and he's the hero with a large scar on his arm from hitting a rock.

He's the hero.

I'm the mad hatter.

Mad.

Mad.

Mad.

The word spins around my head like an ice skater graciously spinning on the ice.

"Please don't leave me."

That was the first thing I remember saying to my dad when I saw him. The nurse thought I was talking to her. I remember her gripping my hand and telling me I was lucky to live.

That's when I sort of died.

I don't remember much else of the big fall. Except it wasn't as big as it looked. The only reason it said no cliff jumping is because there had been sharks spotted in the water weeks before. I guess the sharks missed a pretty delicious meal by avoiding eating me and Nate.

My Nan hasn't been the same since. During the past three weeks, she has pleaded to God for some sort of redemption. This is because she believes her blood is tainted. This is because her son and then granddaughter tried to commit suicide. She knew I didn't trip and fall because she knows me.

"Nesryn?" Lottie says waving her hands in front of my face as I stare off into the distance.

"Yeah." I mumble as Bella holds onto my shoulder.

"Your flight is leaving in a second, I'm going to miss you will you call me and FaceTime every day, I'm going to visit in spring you better be happy when you see me, fuck I'm going to miss you so much!" Lottie says breaking down as I look at her.

"I'm going to miss you too." I mumble quietly trying not to break.

"Promise you won't try to leave again Nesryn I couldn't live with you absent from this earth." Lottie says holding onto me crying. There it is the one thing that held me back before, the one thing I didn't even acknowledge when I tried, the thing that hurts more than the failed attempt, it's the

Guilt.

"I Promise." I say quietly as she kisses Tays cheek.

"Cross your Heart?" She says looking at me as I nod.

"Hope to die." I speak, ironic, right?

"Stick a needle in my eye!" Lottie says giggling giving me one last hug as I wince from the throbbing pain in my stomach.

"Home here we come." Bella says and sighs as I nod.

Hours later.

"Nesryn wake up!" Bella calls hitting my arm over and over again. I groan and open my eyes swinging my arm out to stop her hitting me again.

"The planes landed, look everyone's getting off!" Bella says as I nod and stand up feeling a slight ache in my shoulder remembering the feeling of hitting choppy rocks below me.

I shake away the memory and pick Tay up. I pull my carry-on bag off the shelf and shove it on my back.

"Ready?" I ask, staring at my sister as she nods.

"As I'll ever be!" Bella says sighing. I guess I'm not the only one gutted to be going home to edger and mother.

After a long eight-hour flight, Edger picks us up outside of the airport as I sit in the back of the old beaten-up car twiddling with the bandage around my waist.

"So how was the flight?" Edger says with a chirpy smile on his stupid face.

"It was a flight edger, not a party." I mumble out as Tay laughs at me and I smile at him cheekily.

I got to stay alive.

Not for me.

For them.

For Tay.

"Home sweet home!" Edger chants as I look at my childhood home whilst Edger attempts to park the car without hitting the Mail box.

As me and Bella grab our things and get Tay out of the car, he takes the key out of the ignition.

"Mummy!" Tay speaks excitedly as Bella walks through the door me following slowly behind her.

"Hi my children!" My mother says sounding as nonchalant as ever.

"Oh, you are back as well, Nesryn!" My mother says as I step aside so my mother can see me. She looks me up and down then shoves her glass full of red wine to her chapped lips.

"You've lost weight! "She notes. I nod slowly.

"Thanks." I mumble giving an awkward half smile.

"It wasn't a compliment Nesryn, you need to eat more!" Edger chimes in as I just imagine getting his head and curb stomping him.

"Yes, thank you for your very necessary observation, edger!" I say imagining the second the word edger came out my mouth so did a bullet flying towards his stupid coconut shaped head.

"We need you to watch Tay tonight, we got date night!" My mother says as I nod.

"Bella you too. "my mother says as Bella nods as well.

"He's got a school disco at the community centre at 8pm." My mother announces as me and Bella look at each other.

"It's such a good thing I didn't die huh!" I mumble to myself as my mother glares at me.

An hour later.

Me and Bella are on our way with Tay to the community centre.

"Is that?" I mumble looking at the community centre door as a tall boy with curly golden curls stands.

"Spencer?" I question looking at Bella as she nods.

"Yeah, apparently he just got back from Leeds he had a BMX competition, he did good got to the semi-finals." Bella says as I look at her confused.

"BMX?" I question as she nods.

"Yeah, like small bikes." She says shrugging as I follow her into the community centre.

# CHAPTER TWENTY THREE

Tay runs off as soon as he gets through the door of the community centre as me and Bella stand there looking at each other feeling awkward.

"Well, I need to pee." Bella announces shrugging and walking off.

I sit in one of the small red plastic chairs and watch Tay dance with his little friends as the disco lights flash dimly.

"Nesryn, hi!" Someone says as I stand up and look to where the high-pitched voice is coming from.

"Oh, auntie Lucy, hi it's nice to see you!" I say mumbling my pleasantries like a robot.

"Your cheek, what happened?" Lucy says as I bring my hand up instinctively touching my cheek where the stitch is.

Oh, that. I jumped off a cliff trying to end my life.

"Oh that, my friend's cat scratched me." I mumble as she smiles.

"Your mum told me to meet her here" My aunt says raising her eyebrow. Oh no not my mother lying, it's not like she's never done that before.

"Right, yeah she told me she really wanted to come she's just umm she's ugh she's not feeling well!" I say trying to come up with a lie, aunt Lucy looks at me unconvinced.

"She's not pregnant, is she?" Lucy questions as I chuckle sardonically to myself. It wouldn't surprise me.

"No, she's just got a really severe headache." I mumble as she nods.

"You go find your sister, have fun I will watch Tay, you don't need to always be the adult." Aunt Lucy says as I nod and hug her.

"Thank you." I say smiling a small smile.

"I will take him back to your mother later, you have fun it's a Saturday night." Aunt Lucy announces as I nod.

"Thank you." I say again as she gives me a polite shoo in other words, telling me to leave her alone.

I look around for Bella and remember she needed the toilet.

I walk into the restroom to see her making out with Jared.

"Break it up!" I mumble quietly as she pulls away from Jared's mouth and smirks at me.

"Where's Tay?" She questions whilst holding onto Jared's chest. A ping of loneliness hits me like a bullet to the brain.

"He's with aunt Lucy, said I should enjoy my Saturday night." I say shrugging whilst leaning against the wall.

"That nosy old bat should keep what she thinks to herself!" Bella says crossing her arms as Jared chuckles lowly.

"I want to enjoy myself; I don't want to disappoint her." I announce as Bella rolls her eyes.

The restroom falls silent as I run my hand along the stitch on my cheek.

"You think Nesryn would, do it?" Jared questions looking at Bella, as she shakes her head.

"Nah, she's not like that." Bella says, speaking for me as I look between the two as they smile at each other ominously.

"Nesryn would do what? Nesryn's not like what?" I question as Bella giggles and holds up a tiny bag of what looks like cake topper stickers, the little ones you get with the Peppa Pig fairy cake baking kits.

"I wouldn't eat a sticker?" I say laughing.

"It's acid Nesryn!" Jared says raising his eyebrow as my mouth forms into a shocked circle.

"Right okay, cool cool cool." I say clicking my tongue like it's no big deal, inside I'm completely freaking out.

"So, you want to do it with us?" Bella questions raising her eyebrow. Without a thought or time for hesitation I nod.

"Yep." I mumble as I hold out my hand flat Bella opens the small clear bag, picking the sticker looking tab up.

"Wait, what'd I do with it?" I question as Jared laughs at my native.

"What, I don't know!" I snap glaring at him.

"You just stick it on your tongue and let it dissolve." Bella says as I nod.

She puts the small tab on the palm of my hand and I stick it on my tongue.

"Stick your tongue out girls, say ahh." Jared says as I roll my eyes and Bella does as he says, we both face him with our tongues out chiming, ahhh.

"Perfect." He says smiling as he puts the last tab on his tongue.

I walk out the restroom with Jared and Bella by my side, I look around and the disco-coloured lights have seemed to get brighter.

"Do you see that? It's a cockroach." Bella says as I look down to where she's pointing to but all I see is the floor.

"It's a wooden floor." I say looking at her like she's stupid as her pupils go wide.

"I'm going to dance, come dance, we should dance." Bella mumbles, before I get a chance to detest, she pulls my arm onto the dance area with her.

"Listen it's Bob Marley!" Bella says throwing her hands in the air, but all I hear is baby shark playing and a bunch of small kids guessing and making up the lyrics.

"Bells, it's not Bob Marley." I say tilting my head to the side.

"Shh, you really have to listen, every little thing is gonna be alright." Bella sings as I start to hear the instrumentals of the song.

"I can hear it Bella, I can hear Bob Marley!" I say jumping up and down.

"About a thing, everything little things is gonna be alright!" We shout, swaying our hips as I turn to the side.

"Bella, do you see that? They have red eyes." I mumbled and looked at the parents sitting at the table staring at us.

"Bella!" I mumble, but it looks like she can't hear me.

I groan out loud and make my way towards the door of the community centre.

"Where are you going? You can't leave, you're on acid!" Jared mumbles in my ears as I look up at him and shake my head.

"I'm not planning to leave I just, I need air." I mutter as he nods an approving nod as I glare at him, as if I need his approval.

# CHAPTER TWENTY FOUR

I'm sat outside the community centre with my head in my hands with my eyes shut to avoid seeing the people with red eyes again.

"Nesryn." Someone says as I look up and my eyes catch his.

"Spencer." I say noticing him as I wave a greeting, he comes and sits next to me.

"So, what're you on?" He questions as I scoff.

"I wasn't judging." He says making it clear.

"Acid." I mumble shutting my eyes again as the world feels like it's spinning.

"How'd you get the stitches?" Spencer questions as I sigh.

"You want a lie, or truth?" I question as he smirks.

"I mean you're on acid, it's kinda mandatory for you to tell me the truth including your whole life story." He says smirking as I laugh a tiny bit. The laugh ends up coming out more high pitched than I intended it to.

"I jumped off a cliff to be with my dead dad, after my boss had somewhat consensual sex with me and then told me he didn't like me." I mumble as Spencer takes in a long breath.

"Yeah, I take it back, way too fucked up, you should come up with something like your cat scratched you!" Spencer says as I laugh.

"I did, with my aunt." I announce as he chuckles.

"You remember in computer class, when I'd show you the red album by Taylor Swift and we'd sit and sing together?" I say smiling at him as he nods his head and laughs.

"Ugh, I keep seeing red eyes." I say, shutting my eyes again as Spencer stands up and holds his hand out.

"What are you doing?" I question.

"Come on, I'm taking you to a calm chilled environment where you can enjoy your trip!" Spencer states as I smile and stand up. I take his hand but start to feel a little wobbly again.

"Get on!" Spencer demands seeing me struggling to walk. He's leaning over as I jump on to his back, holding loosely onto his neck.

"We aren't heading to my house; my mother would ride my ass." I mumble as he chuckles.

"Nah, somewhere better!" He says as I smile to myself.

This is thirteen-year-old Me's dream.

"How long, it feels like I've been walking a mile!" I mumble complaining as Spencer chuckles.

"You haven't walked at all look down." He says as I look down and see the floor swaying.

"I'm flying!" I announce contorting my mouth into an O shape and making fish sounds with my tongue against my cheeks.

"No, I'm carrying you." He says as I laugh.

"But I'm like kind of heavy!" I say as he shakes his head.

"You're fine, look we are here!" Spencer announces stepping through a gate.

He lets me down on something.

"A trampoline, your trampoline, I haven't been on this since I was...." I start to say as he interrupts me.

"Thirteen." He says as I climb on. I bounce for a second then stop feeling like the world is spinning.

I drop down laying on the trampoline as Spencer gets on.

He lays with his head to mine; I touch the netting around the trampoline threading my fingers through the intricate circles.

"Want to listen to some music?" Spencer asks as I nod, the warm summer heat hitting my face.

He hands me an ear bud as I pop it into my ear. The smiths start to play as I kick my legs out excitedly.

"We used to love this song, do you remember?" I question excitedly.

"Hell, yeah I do, you remember getting barred from Denny's because we'd sing it so loudly?" He says as I nod proudly remembering.

"Hey Ness, I never got round to saying it, but I'm really sorry your dad died." Spencer says as I hold my breath in staring up at the stars.

"Yeah, me too." I mumble.

"I've missed doing this." I say threading my fingers through his as his fingers circle on the palm of my hand.

"This part always meant so much to me, Nesryn. Did you ever know how much I really liked you?" He questions as my eyes go wide and I wonder if this is real life or if it's altered by the acid trip that I'm having.

"Did you ever know how much I really liked you?" I question sitting up as he does the same.

"I always thought you didn't have time for love." He says as I look down, yes, my depression and lack of father made me avoid human contact, but that didn't mean I didn't crave it.

"You know, if you wanted to, I'd let you have sex with me right here, right now." I announce as I see his eyes glint.

He leans in as I do the same.

I lace my fingers through his golden curls. "I always loved your hair!" I whisper looking at his hair as it literally glows.

He leans in closer, his breath hitches as his lips hug mine; he slowly starts to move his lips in a pattern sequence that makes my heart throb. Letting my hands roam his neck he pulls away and rests his forehead on mine.

"I like you more than to have sex with you here and now." He whispers as I nod and lean into his chest resting my head on his shoulder as I start to slowly cry.

"My dad would've stopped him; he would've told him that I said no, he would've told him that I wasn't ready." I mumble as he strokes my hair.

"It's okay, nothing's going to hurt you, no one's going to hurt you!" He mumbles into my hair as he kisses the top of my hair.

# CHAPTER TWENTY FIVE

thought that I was dreamin'
When you said you love me
The start of nothin'
I had no chance to prepare
I couldn't see you comin'


I wake up in a bed that I don't recognise, I look around to see a photo of Spencer and his cocker spaniel cross poodle. The photo is in a black and silver photo frame sat on top of his bedside table.

I turn to the other side of me to see Spencer sleeping soundly.

I touch his shoulder lightly, "Spencer, I need to go home, Spencer." I call trying to wake him.

I do something completely out of character and lean over close to his ear and spread small kisses on the side of his face.

He lets out small amused chuckles as I smile to myself and lean back.

He sits up as I smile at him.

"Morning sunshine." He says smiling brightly.

Sunshine, that's new.

"Morning." I mumble as Spencer holds my hand under the cover.

"I figured you'd come to the conclusion that I'm a nut case after last night, and chuck me out." I say laughing as he chuckles lightly.

"I probably should've, after showering you because you got yourself so worked up over your scary trip and puked on yourself, I actually came to the conclusion that, yeah this girl is nothing but trouble." He announces as I smirk then stop and look down under the cover.

"You changed me." I mumble.

"It was that or you smelling like yesterday's roast dinner." He says smiling as I narrow my eyes.

"I didn't have roast dinner." I mumble as he chuckles.

"Exactly!" He says as I roll my eyes but feel a small smile poking through.

My phone rings on the bedside table and I lean over and get it.

"Nesryn, mum's pissed you didn't come home, quick come back!"

The text reads as I groan loudly.

"As much as I'm enjoying hearing about my roast smelling puke, my mother seems to be summoning me." I say groaning again as Spencer laughs.

"Maybe we could hangout later, I'm free at three? "He says as I nod.

"Of course, you might have to come to mine though, I'm a half-time mother to my brother." I say as I touch my waist feeling intense pain and aching feeling the healing bruise from falling off the cliff.

"Oh yeah, I changed your bandages they smelt like sick, lucky thing my step dad is a nurse!" He says as I nod.

I lean over and hug him.

"Thank you, I didn't think you even remembered my existence." I mumble as he leans back and looks at me raising his eyebrow.

"How could I ever forget about you, Nesryn?" He says smirking as I laugh.

"Well, I'm glad you didn't." I say holding onto his hand, I let go and get up from the bed.

"I washed your jeans, they're at the bottom of the bed." He says as I nod.

"Thank you." I say smiling a little wider this time.

I pull up my black skinny jeans and look at myself in the mirror. I'm wearing Spencer's oversized nirvana deep grey t shirt resting on top of my jeans.

"I will have this washed by the time we hang out later." I say smiling.

A couple of hours later.

Spencers sat next to me at the dinner table with Bella and Tay opposite us. The room is completely silent, but I feel warmth from Spencer's hand on my thigh.

"So, Spencer you a good guy?" Bella says glaring at him as I kick her under the table.

"You were a couple of grades ahead of me in primary school, you should know." Spencer says as Tay flicks a handful of spaghetti at Spencer, with such grace as Tay smiles widely.

"Oh shit." I mutter looking at the blob of spaghetti on his white t shirt. Spencer laughs along with Tay as they make monster faces at each other.

I stand up as Spencer copies.

"Bells, sit with Tay I'm off to get Spencer his spare top." I mumble as I hold Spencer's hand leading him upstairs.
As soon as we are upstairs, I pull him close to me.

"Want a retry of last night, with less acid?" I say smirking as he nods leaning in and kissing me his lips sliding along mine as a small groan escapes my lips.

I suck on his bottom lip and pull back.

"I can taste spaghetti." I say smirking as he wiggles his eyebrows at me.

"Sexy right?" He says as I nod.

"Mm, very." I say smiling as he pulls me close to him by the bottom of my top.

"We should have sex." I mumble against his lips but he doesn't stop kissing me.

I make my move lifting his top off him, running my hands down his slender torso.

He leans down spreading small sensitive kisses on my neck.

"We should wait, I don't want to fuck things up, Nesryn I really like you." He whispers and pushes a loose strand of my chestnut brown hair behind my ear as I look up at him and nod.

"Will you stay with me, just for tonight? I feel safe with you." I mumble quietly as he nods.

Several hours later.

"Ouch, Nate stop please I thought you loved me ahh." I scream as he pulls my hair roughly crashing into my hips thrusting harder as his eyes go red with lust.

I wake up with a jolt, sitting up abruptly I wipe sweat away from my neck as I look to my left to see Spencer waking.

"Sorry, I don't normally have nightmares." I mumble, I do but they are normally about my father killing himself not Nate.

"It's okay sunshine, nothing's going to hurt you as long as I'm by your side." He says lifting up my top and tracing circles on my back.

# CHAPTER TWENTY SIX

One month later.

Okay next up with has Nesryn's interpretation of where the leaves go?" Mr Rossini says clapping slowly.

I stand up anxiously taking a deep breath as the class watches me. Multiple staring eyes follow me as I walk to the front of the class with my paper in my Shakey hands. I take a small amount of time to breath as I cough a bit and then begin my speech.

"Where do the leaves go? The simple answer is that they fall in heaps piling up on the ground, most likely on the curb, and wind carries most of them away. Winds from the west blow the leaves eastwards, and they catch on anything that blocks their path, including plant life like moss flowers shrubs and grit, some get caught on things like window ledges and fences or hedges but in my opinion they are ultimately on their way to something bigger and better for them much like a caterpillar going through The monumental change of becoming a cocoon then a beautiful elegant butterfly, honestly it would be cynical to think anything else and I'm done being cynical, much like leaves people are ever changing, the colours identical to the makeup we wear, like leaves our greatest glory is not in always falling but, in the reassuring beauty of rising every time we falter ." I speak out coming to an end as the room goes silent and Spencer erupts with cheers as I chuckle and walk, sitting back in my seat.

"Like I said I knew she'd deliver, who's able to top that, any takers?" Mr Rossini says as I smile and look back at Spencer as he winks at me.

I sit through the rest of the class tapping my feet on the floor and daydreaming.

Me and Spencer still haven't had sex yet but that's okay, because he really likes me and I really like him.

He treats me very well, better than I thought anyone could.

The school bell rings loudly and I get up from my seat pulling my backpack up on my shoulder. I make my way to the back of the class, Spencer stands waiting for me with his hand open for me to take.

"Hey." I say smiling.

"Hi." He says turning to face me as he leans in and kisses me.

"Please no PDA, ugh young love disgusts me." Mr Rossini says as I giggle.

"Let's go, you staying with me tonight?" Spencer asks as I look up at him.

"Do you want me too?" I ask as he looks at me and stops walking.

"No Nesryn I asked you because I don't want you too!" Spencer says smirking as I hit his arm playfully.

"Fine, I guess I have too, wouldn't want to disappoint you!" I mumbled as he laughed.

"You remember when we were thirteen and I invited you on my family's boat?" Spencer questions as I think for a second then nod.

"Yeah, Bella told me to date you back then but just because rich men always satisfy a woman's needs her words not mine!" I say smirking remembering the pep talk my sister gave me.

He chuckles and nods. "Well do you want to see the Spencer Express?" Spencer says as I stop walking and look up at him, I burst out laughing.

"You called a boat the Spencer Express, dude that's so conceded!" I say giggling as he nods.

"So, what? You can call me conceded if you want!" He says crossing his arms and pouting his bottom lip out.

"I didn't mean to hurt your very clearly fragile feelings; I'd love to come to see the "Spencer Express!" I say chuckling as he pushes me to the side playfully as I spring back to him and he puts his arm around me.

"Hey Spencer." I say smiling as he drives us to his house.

"Yeah?" He says looking over at me as his hand rests on my thigh.

"I'm really glad you come back into my life." I mumble hoping he doesn't see how embarrassed I am.

"Nesryn, I'm really glad you come back into my boring ass life. I needed some of your sparkle to liven things up." He says as my cheeks flush a bright tomato red colour.

# CHAPTER TWENTY SEVEN

*8 months later*

"Oh my god, Spencer, I mumble feeling him thrust inside me, he holds my hands above my head as his hips rock to Rhythm of his thrusts

"You're so fucking beautiful." He groans in my ear as I hold onto his back for support.

I grind my hips up as he moves in deeper. A scream of pleasure rips through me, as butterflies explode in the deep depth of my stomach.

A deep groan falls from Spencer's mouth as he stills inside me.

"You know since we are getting on the flight tomorrow, I've heard that plane sex is the best kind." Spencer says pulling out of me, lying next to me.

I rest my head in the nape of his neck.

"Mmm I don't know, Bella and Jared's going to be on the flight, what if they hear us." I say looking up at him as he smirks.

"That makes it more fun." He says kissing the top of my head as I giggle.

"well, I mean it's definitely tempting." I say grinning.

"Nesryn, we're home!" My mother calls as I groan and try to get up. Spencer pulls me back down to his chest.

"Stay for a second, lay with me." Spencer says as I giggle.

"We've slept in the same bed for the past seven months Spence." I say smiling as he rolls his eyes, but tightens the grip of his hands around my waist.

"Not nearly as long as I want!" He says looking down at me as I raise my left eyebrow at him.

"How long do you want with me?" I mumble.

"Well, let me think, forever." He says as my cheeks heat, he leans down as I lean up and his lips attach to mine.

"Nesryn we told you we were back!" My mother shouts storming through my bedroom door as I pull away from Spencer shoving the quilt over us.

"Mum, knock always knock!" I hiss out, my cheeks flaming as Spencer hides his face under the cover.

"Umm, sorry I'll wait downstairs till you are done." My mother mumbles.

"Oh, miss Whithorn we finished ten minutes ago!" Spencer announces as my mother's cheeks flame mirroring mine as I shove my hand into Spencer's stomach and he laughs loudly.

24 hours later

"I can't believe I had to cover for you on the plane while you and Spencer were doing god knows what!" Bella snaps glaring at me as we walk ahead to get our luggage whilst Spencer and Jared chat.

"Hey it's not my fault, he wanted to check it off his bucket-list!" I mumble as Bella giggles.

"Lottie!" I shout, noticing my cousin stood at the far end of the airport. Running up to her she jumps into my arms with force as I stumble back a little bit.

"I missed you so much!" I say hugging her as she hugs back.

"Holy, fuck you look amazing!" She announces loudly, smiling sweetly.

"You look gorgeous, this blue is so cool!" I say touching the tips of her blue dyed hair.

"And that must be Spencer, wow he's hot." She says smiling as I giggle.

"This is Aaron, my boyfriend." Lottie says as some guy with black hair walks up to us.

"It's nice to meet you, Aaron." I say smiling as he nods.

"Likewise." He says smiling at us as I feel Spencer's arm snake around my waist protectively.

We are on the drive back home when I see the beach.

"Could you guys drop me off here, I will come home after?" I ask looking at Lottie as she looks at me with concern written on her face.

"Honestly I won't be long at all." I say smiling softly as she nods. I kiss Spencer on the lips as I climb over him to get out the car.

"But what if you're Nan's there? I wanted us to go in together!" He says sounding disappointed as I smile.

"My Nan's at work she will be back at six I will be home by four I promise." I say kissing him again as he nods.

I wait for them to leave as I take a slow walk up the pier making my way to the cliff.

I stand in the exact spot I stopped at when I attempted to fall to my death.

I pull my piece of paper out the back of my black skinny jeans and hold it in my hand.

I look at the suicide note that I wrote the day I was finally ready to end things except for something different, one small but monumental sentence.

I want to live, dad.

I crumble the piece of paper up and fling it into the water. I take a deep breath in and out as I watch the water carry away something that I've held onto this past year.

As I walk back from the pier, I see the souvenir shop I had been to when I wanted to commit suicide the first time I had been here. I shrug and walk into the shop figuring I might as well get Spencer something to remember this trip.

I'm looking at the keychain and postcards when I feel a tap on my shoulder.

"Nesryn." Someone says a voice I haven't heard in a year. I turn around and face him.

"Nate." I mumble, I don't feel sad or angry. It's strange, I don't feel anything.

"How have you been? I haven't seen you around." Nate asks, as I narrow my eyes, why is he making small talk with me, why is he trying to commit to a fair-weather conversation when we both know we hate fair weather talk.

"Thanks, I Umm I actually have to go." I announce trying to sound like I'm in a rush as I grab a post card and a small silver teddy bear keychain.

He says persistently, as I shake my head trying to establish boundaries, "Maybe we could go for coffee. I've really missed you ness, Emma and I got divorced. Say you will come to dinner just the two of us?" I think about answering no, but he insists.

"I don't think that's appropriate Nate, I'm sorry to hear about the divorce, I really am." I say genuinely, as he nods.

"Well, I guess this is it, maybe we could go in my car sometime you know, for old times' sake." He says as I feel like I'm drowning all over again.

"I'm okay, thanks, I've moved on." I mumble handing some cash to the women working the till as he chuckles.

"You always were stubborn that's what I liked about you." He says smirking as I nod internally screaming.

I say, "Well, I hope Lo and Tate are well, and my best wishes are with you." I nod my goodbye to Nate.

After I walk out of the shop and stop, Nate asks, "See you around maybe?".

I am so much better than you, you asshole.

"Goodbye Nate." I say holding my hand out as he shakes it lightly.

"Goodbye Nesryn." He says shaking my hand lightly, then letting go.

A couple hours later.

"Nesryn I think Nan's back!" Lottie says running in my room as me and Spencer sit up on the bed.

"Ready for the beginning of a new chapter, you could always back out now before everything changes?" I say looking at him and noticing how pale he's gone.

"not a chance Nesryn, you're stuck with me" he says standing up off the bed and holding his hand out for me to take.

"Nan, we got something to tell you"

Thank you for reading!

I found the cover art on the internet and edited it to fit the vibe of the book all credit for the cover art goes to the creator : unfortunately I haven't been able to find out who the creater is so no copyright intended, any way I hope everyone enjoyed this book as much as I enjoyed writing it.


Things get better.

Printed in Great Britain
by Amazon

17867943R00123